W9-DEU-111

NIGHTMARE HALL

THE SILENT SCREAM
THE ROOMMATE
DEADLY ATTRACTION
THE WISH
THE SCREAM TEAM

Guilty

In a dark, empty pool . . .

Katie stopped floating, treading water instead, and peered through the darkness for a sign of her roommate. "LuAnn? Is that you?"

A faint swishing sound met her ears. LuAnn was swimming toward her underwater? To surprise her? Scare her?

No. With LuAnn convinced that Katie was only one step away from completely losing her grip, she would never take a chance on pushing her that one extra step by scaring her half to death in a dark, empty pool.

Katie's heart stopped.

Someone *else* was in the water.

Terrifying thrillers by Diane Hoh:

Funhouse

The Accident

The Invitation

The Train

The Fever

Nightmare Hall: The Silent Scream

Nightmare Hall: The Roommate

Nightmare Hall: Deadly Attraction

Nightmare Hall: The Wish

Nightmare Hall: The Scream Team

Nightmare Hall: Guilty

NIGHTMARE HALL

HALL

Guilty

DIANE HOH

SCHOLASTIC INC.
New York Toronto London Auckland Sydney

No part of this publication may be reproduced in whole or in part, or stored in a retrieval system, or transmitted in any form or by any means, electronic, mechanical, photocopying, recording, or otherwise, without written permission of the publisher. For information regarding permission, write to Scholastic Inc., 730 Broadway, New York, NY 10003.

ISBN 0-590-49452-4

12 11 10 9 8 7 6 5 4 3 2 1   3 4 5 6 7 8/9

Printed in the U.S.A.   01

First Scholastic printing, December 1993

NIGHTMARE HALL

Guilty

Prologue

We were all such good friends. Who would have thought it would turn out like this?

It's her fault. She's responsible. And she knows it, no matter what she says. No wonder she's so messed up. Forgetting things, losing things, driving too fast, getting into trouble on and off campus . . . if that's not a guilty conscience, what is?

We all know she's guilty. We pretend we don't, but the truth is there, lying among us, like something rotting. She took something precious from us, and we're all pretending it's okay.

But it's not okay. How could it be? She hasn't been punished.

That's not right. Not right at all.

Something had to be done.

She was given a fair hearing, by the only one of us with guts enough to do it. All of the

1

evidence was weighed carefully. And when that was done, there really was no other choice. She had to be convicted. Because she was guilty. No question about it.

And now the sentence has to be carried out. That's the way justice works, right? Of course, there was only one possible sentence . . .

The death penalty.

Maybe the execution should take place at Nightmare Hall. What could be more perfect? It certainly looks like executions would take place there. Like a prison . . . all that dark brick and those creepy old trees, their black branches hanging down like a hangman's rope. And we've all heard the stories about what happened there . . .

Yes, Nightmare Hall is the perfect place. Perfect. . . .

Chapter 1

Kit was nervous. So many people . . . all gathered in this huge hall for freshman orientation, and she only knew one of them. But Allen, who was Sciences while she was Arts, was on a different line. She saw him over there, casually talking to a big, dark-haired guy wearing glasses. Allen made friends far more easily than she did. It had been that way all through high school. He'd collect them and she'd get to share. It had been a big relief when he'd decided to come to Salem University with her instead of State, as his parents wanted.

He was a good friend to have.

The big guy was cute. Nice smile, well-dressed, in tan pants instead of old cutoffs like most of the guys, and a short-sleeved blue polo shirt. Sunburned face and arms, and *muscles*. Tennis player? Maybe.

I'm dressed all wrong, Kit thought uneasily.

The other girls were wearing shorts and tank tops. She hadn't expected it to be so hot. Almost September, and it was as humid as midsummer. Her white linen blouse scratched her skin, and her black skirt felt like it was made of metal. She should have known better than to wear pantyhose, but her black flats would have felt sticky against bare feet.

What she really wanted to do was run from the crowded, noisy hall and jump into the river that flowed behind the administration building. She had passed it on her way to registration yesterday. It looked cool and tempting — but swift, too. Treacherous current, probably. Not her cup of tea, now that she thought about it. She didn't like deep, swirling water with unknown depths. She preferred the safety of a pool.

Besides, running from a building and jumping, fully dressed, into a rushing river, wasn't the kind of thing Kit Sullivan did. Ever. Good grades, neatness, punctuality, responsibility and reliability, that was Katherine Harrington Sullivan. Ask her teachers. Her parents. Her friends. "Oh, yeah," they'd all say, "you can count on Kit."

Oh, I sound so dull, she thought. No wonder Allen has to find friends for me.

Speaking of . . . here came Allen, towing the

big, dark-haired guy. "Robert Brown, meet Kit Sullivan," Allen said, smiling. Allen was taller than Kit, with gray eyes and pale brows under straight, flat brown hair. He had a thin, triangular face and even white teeth, and a wonderful smile, warm and friendly. Without it, his face could seem stern. But he was seldom without a smile.

"Brownie," the other boy said, grinning down at Kit. "And I think I love you. Will you marry me?"

She could tell he used that line a lot. She hadn't dated much, but she had four brothers. And she might be shy, but she wasn't stupid.

"Sure," she said, tilting her head to look up at him. "What time? Is it okay if I go through orientation first?"

He laughed. To Allen, he said, "I thought you told me she was shy. And you *didn't* tell me her eyes were almost purple."

Kit felt her cheeks flame. Allen had told this total stranger she was shy. He'd probably made her sound like some poor, pathetic reject.

A short, plump, blonde girl accidentally bumped Allen's elbow. "Oops, sorry!" she cried, and then, taking a closer look and seeing Kit, added, "Hey, roomie, how's it going?"

"Fine. LuAnn Price, this is Allen Caine and Robert Brown."

"Brownie. You're roommates?"

Kit nodded. She had only seen LuAnn for a minute or two, in their room in the Quad . . . four tall stone buildings linked by an area of green known as the Commons. They had introduced themselves, LuAnn had tossed four plaid suitcases in a corner, said "Bye!" and left the room.

Kit had stayed behind and carefully, methodically, unpacked.

"So, are you 'oriented' yet?" LuAnn cracked, smiling up at Brownie.

A flirt. Good. Maybe she gave lessons.

"Not yet," he answered. "I'm hunting for my sister. She's a sophomore, but she's helping out here today. Caroline Brown. Callie. Tall, lots of hair, same color as mine, looks like she could tame wild tigers. There she is, over there." He waved a hand. "Hey, Callie, get over here and give us some tips." A tall girl in shorts and a red T-shirt broke away from a group and made her way to Brownie's side.

"So, you made it, after all! Dad will faint. He was sure you'd skip out and wander around the country for the next nine months. Introduce me to these unfortunate people who must be friends of yours."

Kit liked Callie instantly. She had a fresh, open look about her, and her affection for her brother was evident in the way she smiled at him.

Maybe this "Brownie" person was worth knowing.

They were all told to take seats, then. LuAnn quickly grabbed a chair on one side of Brownie. And Kit surprised herself by taking the other. Callie, she noticed, stood slightly off to one side, smiling, deliberately letting Kit ease in front of her.

Kit flashed Brownie's sister a smile of thanks. And decided that even if it turned out that Brownie wasn't worth knowing, Callie definitely was.

They both were, Kit learned over the next few wonderful weeks. Callie, Kit, and Brownie, joined by a friend of Callie's, a sophomore named Davis Teale who quickly became Brownie's best friend, and Allen and LuAnn went everywhere together: dances, parties, orientation gatherings, hiking at a nearby state park, movies, football games, and swim meets. They gathered at Vinnie's, a popular pizza restaurant in the town of Twin Falls, and talked and laughed and, occasionally, sang along with the jukebox. They met at Burgers Etc., a long, silver diner midway between the campus and the town for lunch or late at night. Sometimes they argued: politics, religion, philosophy. Kit was always astonished to hear herself voicing an opinion. But it felt good, and no one ever told her she didn't know what she was talking about.

They studied together evenings, sometimes at Dennison Memorial Library on campus, sometimes at an off-campus dorm down the highway, Nightingale Hall, where one of LuAnn's new friends, Linda Carlyle, lived. They were both on the swim team, and got along well.

Nicknamed "Nightmare Hall" because a girl had killed herself there — or so it was said — Kit had at first been intimidated by the place. Old, isolated at the top of a hill, and heavily shaded by a thicket of huge old oak trees, it definitely looked haunted.

But sitting on a worn Persian carpet in front of a roaring fireplace in Nightingale Hall's library, surrounded by her new friends and bowls of popcorn and yogurt-covered raisins, with Brownie at her side, any feeling of uneasiness Kit had felt upon entering the gloomy foyer disappeared.

And her happiness grew.

On Saturday nights they often drove into town to Hunan Manor for a Chinese dinner. Kit's favorite part was opening the fortune cookies.

"Well, how about that?" she cried on one of these excursions. She held out the small piece of paper for Brownie to read. "I'm going to be rich!"

He read it aloud. *"Follow your heart and fortune will follow you."*

"Fortune?" Allen said. "That means money, right?"

Brownie smiled at Kit. "Right. But first, you have to follow your heart." He took her hand in his under the table.

"No problem," she said lightly, returning the smile.

She wanted the evening to go on forever.

But they had plans to go hiking the following day. And when LuAnn's fortune cookie read, *A wise heart sings at the sunrise*, they laughed and made it an early night.

Brownie's kiss that night was soft and sweet.

"You're so lucky," LuAnn said when they were in bed with the lights out. "Everybody likes Brownie. There isn't a girl on campus who wouldn't trade places with you."

And if Kit heard in LuAnn's voice that no one understood why popular, outgoing, life-of-the-party Brownie had picked quiet, efficient, responsible Kit Sullivan over prettier, more popular, fun-loving girls, she didn't care. It didn't matter. Because he *had* picked her.

She'd stopped trying to figure out why.

Davis had said once, "Why not? Why not you? You're gorgeous, you must know that. Liz Taylor, when she was young. You have the same eyes. And Brownie doesn't *need* a life-of-the-party girl." Davis laughed. "He'd hate the competition, for one thing." Then he'd added, more seriously, *"You're* what Brownie needs. And he's smart enough to know that. Callie says, 'Thank God!' "

And silently, to herself, Kit had said the same thing.

Now, she fell asleep content with the thought that she'd be spending the next day with Brownie. And the weather was supposed to be beautiful.

It was. It was one of those perfect gold and scarlet and orange blue-skied days that tricks people into forgetting that winter is not far away. In the golden glow of autumn, with a warm, gentle breeze stirring the brilliantly colored leaves, the cold, harsh reality of winter seemed comfortably distant.

But Kit's pleasure in the perfect day faltered when they reached the canoe landing on the swiftly flowing river behind the university. Recent rains had raised the river's level and widened it considerably. Brownie had planned a canoe ride, and Kit had agreed. But that was before she'd seen the change in the muddy brown water. It seemed to her that it made an ominous sucking sound as it rushed past the embankment where they were standing.

"Brownie, I don't know . . ." she said hesitantly. "It's going so *fast!*" She glanced around her for confirmation from their friends. But Callie had already led Allen, Davis, and LuAnn on a hike along the riverbank. She had borrowed Brownie's camera. They were all going to meet later at the bridge in the center of Twin Falls.

Brownie flexed his biceps. "C'mon, Kit, we can't let this muddy old river get the best of us. We *like* challenge, right?"

She forced a weak laugh. "Brownie, I don't swim that well. I mean, I love it, but . . . in a *pool*, where I can touch bottom if I have to."

"Who said anything about swimming? You think I can't handle this river? Would I let you end up in the drink?" He bent down and untied one of several canoes kept at the landing for students and faculty. "Have faith, Kit, have faith."

At least two other canoes were missing. That reassured Kit. Didn't that mean other people thought the river was safe? They wouldn't be the only people on the water.

That was good.

And Brownie was so determined. He seemed so confident that they'd be safe.

So, the ever-cautious, ever-careful Kit Sullivan put one foot into the canoe, bending to hold the edges with her hands, and then she put the other foot in.

Brownie pushed the canoe away from the riverbank and jumped in, grinning at Kit as he picked up an oar.

The little boat was immediately caught up in the swirling torrent and carried along at an amazing speed. Kit sat quietly, afraid to move a muscle. The canoe suddenly seemed so light, so fragile, in the wide span of rushing brown water.

When she looked over at Brownie, sitting opposite her, she knew by the look on his face that he'd realized his mistake. Too late. His jaw was clenched, his knuckles white. He paddled furiously, but it was hopeless. They might as well have been in a paper boat.

Kit's teeth began to chatter. No one else was on the river. Those other canoes hadn't been taken out by other people. They'd probably been torn from their moorings by the violent tug of the water.

"At this rate," Brownie shouted over the river's roar, "we'll be at . . . the bridge . . . long before the others!" But his face was white.

Kit had never imagined that Brownie could be scared. She, yes. Many things scared her. But not Brownie.

She reached out then, to touch his hand, tell him that it would be okay. But before her hand met his, Brownie shouted an oath. The canoe was headed straight for a huge tree limb jutting up out of the water.

"Hold on!" he shouted, paddling furiously.

It was hopeless. The canoe slammed full force into the tree. Kit and Brownie, their faces white with fear, clutched the sides of the small boat. It bounced backward, tilted dangerously and then, just when they thought it would right itself, toppled over onto its side in the water.

They cried out as, reaching for each other, they were tossed into the muddy, swirling water.

Chapter 2

Cold . . . the water was so cold. It filled her mouth and nose. She spat it out, but more rushed in. Down, down . . . the dark, muddy water closed over her. It was heavy, heavy and so strong, tugging at her, swirling her, pushing. . . .

She was yanked to the surface, coughing and gasping, by a strong arm. Brownie . . . his curly hair sodden, his face grim.

The canoe was gone, hurtling down the river, just out of reach ahead of them.

They had nothing to hold on to.

"I can't . . . I can't . . ." Kit gasped, clutching Brownie's shirt.

"I've got you," he told her. "Let me do it. Put your arms around my neck and go limp, okay? I'll get you to shore, I promise."

She did as he told her.

In the safety of a swimming pool, Kit had

thought of water as kind, gentle, soothing.

But not this water. This water was cold and cruel, and it meant them harm.

Brownie fought valiantly, but for every stroke he took toward the river's banks, the water's force yanked him backward. The current seemed determined to keep them in its deathly grip.

We're not going to make it, Kit thought. Brownie was fighting so hard. But she could feel him tiring. And the river tugged at her arms around his neck, intent on ripping her free.

If she tried to make it on her own, Brownine might have a chance. It was her weight on his back that was making it so hard for him.

But she couldn't let go. She couldn't. He could make it without her. But she'd never make it without him.

"I'm sorry," she whispered in his ear, knowing he couldn't hear her over the rushing water. "I'm sorry, Brownie." As they were swept under the stone bridge in the center of Twin Falls, a cold and exhausted Kit was vaguely aware of shouts from above.

Help . . . the people on the bridge would get help. Someone would come to get them out of the river.

Brownie fought to keep them from slamming

into the thick stone pillars supporting the bridge.

The shouts from the bridge meant that help was on its way. If Brownie could just keep them afloat a few more minutes . . .

They would be safe on dry land soon.

But she was so tired. She couldn't hang on any longer. It would be so easy to let go, to slide down into the deep, murky water and let it swallow her up.

As if he had sensed her thoughts, Brownie gasped, "Hang on . . . almost there . . . hang on . . ."

And a moment later, they were lying in calmer water close to the riverbank. Here, the embankment curved, creating a small, peaceful pocket. Brownie, his eyes alert for a way out, had spotted the tiny inlet and struggled toward it.

Too exhausted to speak, Kit slid off Brownie's back and stumbled over to the shore, where she collapsed. Her eyes closed, she lay on her stomach, half-in, half-out of the water. Her face rested on cool, smooth mud . . . proof that they had made it to land.

They were out of that angry, noisy water.

They were safe.

But when she reached out with one arm to

touch Brownie, her fingers sank into nothing but oozing mud.

Her eyes flew open.

Brownie wasn't there.

Kit bolted upright, whirled to face the water.

And heaved a sigh of relief. There he was, still floating in the inlet. A wave of guilt assailed her. He'd been too tired from hauling her on his back to make his way to shore.

She should have stayed behind and helped him instead of making her way to safety alone. But she had thought he was right alongside her the whole time.

"Brownie?" she called, wading back into the water. It seemed even colder than before. "Are you okay?"

He waved a hand in response.

"I'm coming out to help you!" She began wading through the waist-high water to where he lay, on his back, at the edge of the inlet. "It's not safe out there!"

A long time after that day, Kit would remember saying that, and she would wish with a fierce passion that she hadn't been right.

But she *was* right.

She was only a few feet away from Brownie, struggling to maintain her balance in deeper water, when a sudden swirl of the rushing river tugged at Brownie, yanking him free of the inlet, pulling him, so quickly that Kit barely had time to blink, back into the current.

Startled to find himself suddenly back in the river's clutches, Brownie cried out. His arms began flailing wildly as Kit, watching in horror, screamed his name.

She was still screaming when, trying desperately to swim, Brownie was swept out into the middle of the river and, a second later, disappeared around a bend.

Chapter 3

TWIN FALLS: *The body of an eighteen-year-old freshman at Salem University has been recovered in the Salem River following an intensive search. The student, Robert Xavier Brown, of Valley Ridge, New York, was canoeing on the rain-swollen river on Sunday afternoon with a fellow student when their craft overturned. After saving the life of his companion, whose name has not been released, Mr. Brown was swept back out into the river and drowned.*

Mr. Brown is survived by his parents, Carl and Julia Brown of Valley Ridge; a sister, Caroline, also a student at Salem, and a brother, Stefan.

A memorial service for Mr. Brown will be held at ten o'clock Wednesday morning in the Tyler Chapel on the campus of Salem University.

Chapter 4

Room 236 in the Quad was a mess. Both beds were unmade and blanketed with a jumble of bedding, books, papers, and notebooks. The floor was littered with discarded clothing. Every flat surface was piled high with more books and notebooks, makeup, jewelry, socks and scarves and hats, combs and brushes, and boxes of tissues. A large, blue plastic wastebasket in the corner was spilling over, the overflow around its base a messy collection of crumpled papers, used cotton balls, and makeup remover pads, and empty plastic snack bags.

"This place is a pigsty," LuAnn commented in disgust as she came out of the bathroom, a towel wrapped around her head. "I've *always* been a slob, but you used to be so neat, Kit. Don't you *ever* hang anything up anymore?"

"I told you not to call me that," her roommate snapped. "I told *all* of you. If you don't call me Katie, I'm not going to answer you." She was standing in front of the dresser mirror, scrunching her newly permed dark hair into a mass of curls. "And I *meant* it, LuAnn."

LuAnn sighed and sat down amid the clutter on her bed. "Okay, okay. But it's hard. I mean, I *met* you as Kit. I *think* of you as Kit. Everyone does. We're having a hard time remembering."

Katie Sullivan applied bright pink lipstick with a heavy touch. "People get new nicknames all the time. Especially at college. New place, new life, why not a new name? It's no big deal."

"But — "

Lipstick in hand, Katie whirled. "It's *no* big deal, LuAnn. Besides, it's been a whole month since I told you not to call me Kit anymore. You should have it down by now."

"I know," LuAnn admitted. "It was right after . . ." she faltered, her voice breaking off abruptly.

"Never mind," Katie said brusquely, turning back to the mirror. But her hands shook as she worked on her hair, and unshed tears glittered in her eyes.

After a few silent moments, LuAnn said hesitantly, "Well, could we maybe straighten things up a little bit before you go out? It's not like I'm a neat freak or anything, Ki . . . Katie, but we can't *walk* in this room without tripping over something."

"Go ahead and straighten all you want." She applied two coats of mascara to her thick curly eyelashes. "But if you ask me, life is too short to waste any part of it doing boring things like cleaning. Boring, boring, boring!"

"You study and write papers," LuAnn pointed out. "That's boring."

"Not always. Anyway, I do it because I want to stay in school. So I don't have any choice. But," glaring at the mess on the floor, "if they kicked us out for sloppy rooms, the dorms would be emptied faster than a sinking ship."

The expression had a disastrous effect. Ship . . . sinking . . . water . . .

Canoe overturning . . . the river . . .

Katie went white, and had to clutch the edge of the dresser for support.

Tears welled up in LuAnn's eyes. "Oh, Katie," was all she could manage. She got up and moved to put an arm around her roommate.

But Katie quickly took a deep breath and whirled away from LuAnn. "Look, I've got to go," she said briskly. "Allen's waiting. See you later, okay? Don't wait up!"

"I never do. I know better."

Katie grabbed a jacket from one of the floor

piles and tossed it on over her jeans and bright red sweater.

"I don't know how you do it," LuAnn said as Katie grabbed her purse. "Staying out so late, hardly eating anything, not sleeping. You have those awful nightmares almost every single night. Don't you get *tired*?"

"Life is too short to get tired," was the answer that floated over Katie's shoulder as she hurried from the room. "*Much* too short!"

Twenty minutes later, at Burgers Etc., Callie and Davis joined Allen in urging Katie to "eat something."

"You must be running on pure adrenaline," Davis remarked, watching Katie push her hamburger back and forth on her plate with the fork she had thrust into its middle. "I haven't seen you chew and swallow anything in weeks."

"Are you guys almost done?" she asked impatiently. "You've been eating for *hours*. We're going to be late for the movie."

"Relax!" Allen cautioned, frowning at her. "We've got plenty of time. Boy, you can't sit still for five minutes anymore."

"Allen . . ." Callie warned.

Katie saw the look that passed between the two, and burned with humiliation. Taking care of her . . . they were still taking care of her. Watching what they said, careful not to mention Brownie's name around her, never talking about that day . . .

They had all said the same thing: "It wasn't your fault."

If it wasn't her fault, why didn't they talk about it when she was around?

It *wasn't* her fault. It couldn't be. She couldn't bear that . . .

"I have to get out of here!" she cried and, grabbing her jacket, ran from the diner. She could feel the stares as she pushed open the door, could almost hear the whispers . . .

"That's the girl Brownie saved from the river. That's what killed him, you know . . . saving *her*." Ever since she came back, people had been staring at her on campus, looking at her as if she were an oddity. She couldn't tell whether they blamed her for the loss of Brownie, their friend, or if they thought the loss had unhinged her and were waiting for her to shatter into a thousand tiny pieces.

She had thought there were no more tears inside of her, that every last drop of saltwater had already been spent. But, standing outside the diner with no place to go, fresh tears began to warm her cheeks.

Then Davis's voice said, "Katie. . . ."

She turned and buried her face in his chest. "I miss him so much," she whispered. "Sometimes I just can't stand it, it hurts so bad."

"I know," he said. He put comforting arms around her. "We all miss him."

She heard the comment as blaming, and jerked backward, crying out, "It wasn't my fault! The river . . ."

"I know that, Katie," Davis said quietly. "Calm down."

She couldn't talk about this. "I know what," she said with false cheer, "let's skip the movie and go dancing! It'll be more fun. The movie sounds boring, anyway."

Callie and Allen exited the restaurant and caught the last part of Katie's statement.

"We *planned* on a movie, Katie," Allen argued. "I don't feel like dancing."

"I don't, either," Callie agreed. "And a nice, quiet movie would be good for you, Katie. You need to relax."

"I don't *want* to relax! Relaxing is a colossal waste of time." Katie glanced from face to face. "Doesn't *anybody* want to go dancing? Davis?"

He shook his head no.

She was driving, and could have refused to take them to the theater in the mall.

But then Callie and Davis would give her that look she hated — the one that said, "Here she goes again." And Allen would say, "Since when are you so hot for dancing? You've always liked movies better."

It wasn't worth arguing about. "Okay, okay, the movie it is. But it better not be boring."

She couldn't have said afterward if it was boring or not. Because she couldn't concentrate on the story. It seemed to have something to do with outer space. She couldn't sit still, and was continually leaving her seat to buy soda or Milk Duds or popcorn. She ate none of it. But leaving her seat to go to the concession stand was something to *do*.

They were all very annoyed with her for bouncing up and down like a yo-yo.

And she was annoyed with *them* for being annoyed with *her*.

And then, when they reached her car, sitting under a pole light in the parking lot, Allen complained that it was filthy.

"Look at that!" he said, clearly disgusted. "Where have you been driving that thing? Don't you ever wash it?"

She didn't tell him she often drove it, late at night, along the dirt road behind campus that wandered alongside the river. The road was always muddy. She didn't care. She drove to the spot where she and Brownie had stepped into the canoe, and parked. Sometimes she sat there, alone, for hours.

She would have lost her temper then, something she did quite often now, and yelled at Allen that if he didn't like riding in a dirty car, he could walk. But just then Callie said, "What is *that?*" Her eyes were focused on the hood of Katie's car.

"What's the matter?" Davis asked, moving closer to Callie to look where she was looking. And said, "Oh . . ."

The two of them tried to block Katie's view then, pushing in front of her, but her curiosity had been aroused. She made an end run around them to check out the hood.

Written in the dust, in large, sloppy but clearly legible letters was one word: *GUILTY*.

Chapter 5

They all stared silently at the message fingered into the dried mud on Katie's car.

Allen broke the silence by saying, "A simple 'WASH ME' would make more sense."

Well, yes . . . *if* the message referred to her dirty car. But what if it *didn't*?

Davis asked, "Have you . . . is this the first time someone's sent you this kind of message?"

Katie knew what he meant. *He* wasn't so sure the message referred to her dirty car, either.

She nodded. No other messages. This was the first.

And the last?

Maybe. Maybe not . . .

After the accident, everyone, including Callie, who had lost her brother, had said, "It's not your fault." True, she had screamed at Katie that day, when she first found out that

Brownie was missing. The words were burned into Katie's brain. "Why did *you* get out safely?" Callie had cried, tears streaming down her face. "Why *you*, and not him?" But she had apologized later, after they'd all come back to school. And they had cried together and then it had been okay between them. And Callie had said more than once since then, "It's not your fault. It was an accident."

Katie's eyes returned to the dusty message. Maybe there was someone who disagreed.

"They've got some nerve, making a mess on your car like that," Callie said, and climbed into the backseat.

In the car, as Katie, unnerved, fumbled to start the car, Allen warned, "Don't make a big deal out of this, okay? Some jerk walking by thought it would be fun to rattle someone's cage. He probably didn't even know whose car is *was*."

Possibly. Except . . . except no one else on campus drove an orange Honda with a license plate that read, simply, KIT-18. Her stepfather had bought her the car *and* the special license plate for her eighteenth birthday.

Maybe the author of her message hadn't even noticed the license plate. It was probably too dirty to read, anyway.

Allen was right. The message was a random

one, not meant for anyone special. Not meant for *her*.

She'd wash the car tomorrow, first thing.

"So," she said brightly as they headed for campus, "who's up for dancing now?"

"Katie!" Callie wailed. "I'm tired, and I've got a psych test to study for. Give me a break!"

Katie glanced in the rearview mirror. "Davis? Come on, you love to dance."

"True. But not when I've got a tennis match the next day. Some other time, okay?"

"That's not fair," Katie complained. "I went to your boring movie."

"How would you know if it was boring or not?" Allen said irritably. "You weren't in your seat long enough to judge. And you should get some sleep. You look like you haven't slept in weeks."

Thirty-eight days exactly, Katie answered silently. Aloud, she said, "Allen, you silver-tongued devil, ease up on the flattery. A girl can't think straight."

Davis laughed.

"Sorry," Allen muttered. "I just meant . . ."

"I *know* what you meant." She had mirrors in her room. Allen was right. He was the only one honest enough to tell her that she looked like death warmed over.

Death. . . .

"I'm *going* dancing tonight," she announced frantically, and pressed down on the accelerator, speeding up the highway toward campus until Callie protested so loudly, Katie was forced to slow down.

"You're going to get another ticket," Allen warned.

She'd had two in the past four weeks. They were still in the glove compartment, silent yellow reminders of her lawbreaking.

"You never *used* to drive too fast," Allen added accusingly. To the backseat, he said, "In high school, everyone called her Pokey Joe because she was so cautious."

"Well, that was then and this is *now*," Katie snapped. "Live with it."

She was sorry immediately, but it was too late to take it back. That happened a lot lately. It was amazing that she had any friends left at all.

When they reached campus, still alive with Friday-night activity, they gathered around the fountain on the Commons, trying to talk Katie into calling it a night.

"But it's *early*!" she protested, flopping down on the low stone wall around the fountain. A spray of cold water chilled her cheek as she turned sideways.

If she went back to the room, she was so

tired she'd probably fall asleep. And then she'd have the nightmare . . . the horrible, sickening dream of Brownie floating, lifeless, in that cold and muddy water, his curly brown hair splayed out around him, his eyes open, staring, unseeing . . .

And then she'd wake up screaming, and LuAnn would rush over to comfort her but wouldn't know the right words to say.

Because there *weren't* any.

"I'm *not* going to bed!" she cried.

Before anyone could argue with her, a couple passed by the fountain carrying a small portable radio, playing bright, lively music.

"Hey, wait!" Katie cried impulsively, "let me borrow that for a minute? I'll give it right back, I promise."

Looking uncertain, the girl extended the radio.

"Set it right here on the wall, okay?"

The radio was positioned next to her. The couple stood back then, watching with interest.

Katie looked directly at Allen. "I *said* I was going dancing, and I *meant* it!" And, pushing off her sneakers, she jumped into the fountain and began dancing in the water, singing along with the radio.

The radio's owners laughed. But Allen said,

"Katie, get *out* of there! You're going to get us all in trouble."

People walking across the night-darkened campus were drawn to the music and began moving toward the fountain.

"Katie . . ." Callie began, but Katie's response was to sing louder.

The water was very cold. It came to her knees. Her jeans and her socks were sodden, her fingers icy from the spray and her splashing. Although she was aware of the crowd gathering around the fountain, her mind kept flitting back to the ugly word scrawled on the hood of her car.

GUILTY.

I'm not, she thought, still singing along with the radio as she frolicked in the fountain, I'm *not* guilty. Everyone said so, everyone said it wasn't my fault.

But. . . . Brownie was still gone. Dead. Drowned.

"Katie, come on out of there," Callie begged.

"You'll get pneumonia," Allen called. "You're soaked, and it's cold out."

Katie laughed. "What are you guys, my parents? I'm just dancing. Since when is there a law against dancing?"

The people gathered around the fountain began clapping in time to the music. A trio of boys urged her on, shouting, "Go, girl, go!"

Someone turned the radio up. Several loud voices began singing. Callie begged Katie again to leave the fountain.

Katie, splashing, dancing, singing, her curly wet hair frizzing around her face, turned her head to look at Callie, and wondered why Brownie's sister didn't hate her.

I would hate me if I were her, she thought, and slipped, and fell. Her legs went out from under her, and suddenly she was sitting in the water.

It was very cold.

And then arms were lifting her up, and out of the fountain, and Davis's voice in her ear was saying quietly, "Okay, Katie, that's it, let's go get you dried off."

She was shivering uncontrollably. Davis took off his jacket and wrapped it around her, but it didn't help.

The radio was silenced, and the crowd began to thin. Katie heard someone mutter, "That Katie! She'll do anything for a laugh."

And someone else replied, "Yeah, like Brownie. No wonder they were nuts about each other. Two of a kind, if you ask me."

But we *weren't* two of a kind, Katie protested silently as Davis hurried her along the Commons. I wasn't *like* Brownie. Not then.

People didn't write a word like "guilty" on a dirty car unless they had a reason. They wrote WASH ME.

Did someone out there think she was guilty of something?

What did they think she was guilty of?

As if she didn't know.

She had never in her life felt so cold.

Chapter 6

Katie couldn't get warm. At Callie's urging, she had taken a hot shower. Then she'd slipped into warm, fleecy sweats and buried herself beneath the covers on her bed. But it was no use. She couldn't stop shaking, and her teeth were chattering furiously.

She had sent Allen, Callie, and Davis away, back to their own rooms. They hadn't wanted to go. They were worried about her. But she could see that their concern was mixed with disapproval over what Allen called her "stupid stunt."

LuAnn wasn't sympathetic, either. "Well, it's your own fault. I couldn't believe it when Allen told me how you got so wet." She shook her head. "I thought I had such a levelheaded roommate. Now, I wonder. Everyone on campus is going to think I'm rooming with a nut case."

"Maybe you are," Katie bit out from between her chattering teeth.

LuAnn had been patient with the sudden changes in her roommate since Brownie's death. She had been sweet and understanding, even though she, too, missed Brownie.

But she had been in the front seat of the orange Honda the day that Katie, ignoring the speed limit, had narrowly missed a small cocker spaniel crossing the road. And she'd been sitting in the same seat when Katie was stopped by a police officer later that same day and given a ticket for speeding, along with a stern lecture. LuAnn had been more upset by the episode than Katie.

She'd also been awakened from a sound sleep on more than one occasion in the early hours of the morning by the sound of Katie's key turning in the lock.

Add to that the messy room and the constant music that Katie played in an effort to keep from hearing her own thoughts, and LuAnn had just about lost all patience with her roommate.

Katie couldn't blame her.

"I'm going up to Nightingale Hall to see Linda," LuAnn said, tossing a red windbreaker over her denim shirt. "She invited me to sleep over, and I might. So don't worry if I don't come back, okay? Get some sleep, Katie." The door closed after LuAnn with a sharp click.

Katie lay awake, shivering in the darkened room. They would talk about her, LuAnn and her friend Linda, and the other students who lived at Nightingale Hall. Nightmare Hall . . . LuAnn must like Linda a lot, to be willing to spend the night in that place. It wasn't bad inside, especially when there were roaring fires in the fireplaces. But from the outside, it looked really creepy, so dark and gloomy with all those big old trees hiding it from the sun, and the porch tilting slightly, as if it had had one too many. Jessica Vogt and Ian Banion, who lived there, seemed to like it. But there were rumors that some girl had died there, which didn't surprise Katie at all. It *looked* like the kind of place where people died.

At Nightmare Hall, they would all talk about her . . . LuAnn's crazy roommate. Wasn't even safe to sleep in the same room with her, because she woke up screaming all the time. Besides, you just never knew what she might do next, did you?

People had said the same thing about Brownie. But they hadn't thought he was crazy. They'd thought he was fun.

I must not be doing it right, Katie thought, huddling deeper within the comforter.

LuAnn was right about one thing: jumping into that fountain had been a stupid thing to do. Getting soaked like that, in water so cold . . . She had already missed two weeks of school . . . after the accident.

Her parents had talked her into going back to Salem. "Brownie wouldn't want you to quit school," they had argued while she sat on a kitchen stool, her head down, crying. "From what you've told us about him, he'd want you to continue."

She knew they were right.

She'd missed a lot of classes. Callie had, too, but Callie wasn't going around jumping into fountains and not sleeping half the night. Callie was "catching up." If I get sick because of this, Katie scolded herself, I'll never get caught up. And the whole semester will go up in smoke.

How could she have been so stupid?

"You need to loosen up," he said, smiling down at her. "Life isn't that scary, Kit. You're so cautious, so careful. What are you afraid of?"

"Practically everything," she admitted, and wondered if he realized that she wasn't kidding.

"You have to jump into life with both feet,"

he said, taking her hands in his. "To show the world that you're not afraid. It's the only way to live."

And so she had tried. Because it seemed to work so well for Brownie. He had so many friends, had so much fun. She had tried to be more like him.

But she hadn't perfected it fast enough, had she? Not enough to keep her from panicking in that angry brown water.

Not her fault. Anyone would have been afraid. Even Brownie . . . she had seen it in his face.

Not her fault. Everyone said so. Her friends, her parents, the counselor on campus who offered grief counseling to those who needed it. . . . all of them had said the same thing: "It was an accident."

Well, yes, of course it was.

But thinking that didn't bring Brownie back, did it?

Campus seemed so . . . all *wrong*. . . . without him.

Davis had accused her of trying to fill the gap left by Brownie's absence. While he was helping her into the dorm, he had said, "You don't have to prove anything, Katie. Not to anyone. No one expects you to take Brownie's place. No one except you."

Well, if that was what she was trying to do, she wasn't doing it very well.

Maybe the word GUILTY on her car had simply meant that she was guilty of acting like an idiot.

Had the person who wrote that later watched as she splashed around in the fountain? If he had, he'd probably write CRAZY the next time.

And maybe he'd be right.

She fell asleep crying quietly.

It was still pitch-black in the room when she was yanked out of sleep by a sound.

What sound? Had LuAnn changed her mind about staying over at Nightmare Hall and come home, after all?

I wouldn't blame her, Katie thought sleepily, sitting up. Who'd want to spend a night in that place if they didn't have to? Such a dark and gloomy house . . .

"LuAnne?" Katie called. "Is that you?"

There was no answer.

The building was quiet. No music, no sound of running water, no footsteps hurrying down the hall, no elevator hum. Katie glanced at her illuminated alarm clock. Three A.M. No wonder it was so quiet. LuAnn wouldn't have left Nightmare Hall this late to come back to the dorm, so that couldn't be what had awakened her.

Besides, LuAnn would have answered when Katie called her name.

"LuAnn?" Katie repeated.

Silence. Total, utter silence, in the darkened room.

But she had heard *something*. A door slamming? The brakes on a car screeching, as someone raced back to campus after a long night out?

And then the voice ended the silence.

"It's all your fault!"

A male voice, clearly recognizable.

Katie gasped and clutched the comforter close to her chest. No. She couldn't have heard that. Not possible . . .

"It's all your fault!" the same voice said again.

Shrinking back against the wall, Katie felt her blood turn to ice. Her breath caught in her chest. She knew that voice. She would never forget the sound of it, not for the rest of her life. She often heard it in her sleep.

"It's all your fault!" came a third time.

A wave of dizziness engulfed her. I'm asleep, she told herself, I'm still asleep. I only think I'm sitting up, awake. I have to be asleep, because I can't be hearing what I'm hearing, I can't be, it's not real, it can't be real. . . .

Again she heard, *"It's all your fault!,"* and she moaned, her hand over her mouth to keep from screaming.

Because the voice she heard was unmistakably Brownie's.

Chapter 7

Over and over, again and again, as Katie sat, frozen and mute on the bed, Brownie's voice repeated the cruel phrase, "It's all your fault."

It seemed to go on forever.

Finally, it ended. The darkened room filled up with silence again.

But Katie didn't move. She couldn't. She sat huddled against the wall, buried in the comforter, trembling with shock and fear.

That voice . . . she would know that voice anywhere. It was deep, confident, warm. Except when he was annoyed . . .

"Why don't you want to go to the party?" he demanded. *"We talked about it, we planned to go, now you say you're too tired."*

"Well, I am. We go out every single night, and I have studying to do and laundry to do, and Brownie, there just isn't enough time to do everything!"

"Let the laundry go. They're not gonna put on your tombstone, 'This girl did a great laundry.' Wouldn't you rather they put, 'This girl knew how to have a good time'?"

"But . . ."

"I keep telling you, kitten, loosen up! You worry too much. Life is short."

She had gone to the party. And she'd had a wonderful time. And two weeks later, she'd found out that Brownie was right. Life was short. Too short . . .

She was still sitting in the same position, her back against the wall, the comforter pulled up to her chin, her eyes wide, her lower lip trembling, when LuAnn came in shortly after seven-thirty.

"I'm never going to make my eight o'clock . . . Katie, what's wrong?"

Katie's eyes moved to LuAnn. If she told LuAnn what she'd heard, LuAnn would tell her she'd been dreaming. She would say emphatically that it *had* to be a dream. She couldn't possibly have heard Brownie talking to her.

LuAnn would say, "Well, of course you were asleep, Katie. It just *seemed* real."

Anyone with half a brain would say that. Davis would. And Callie. And especially sensible Allen.

Well, if everyone *else* would see it as a

dream, why couldn't she? If she could believe it had been a dream, she wouldn't have to tell anyone. And no one would know she was hearing things. Things that she couldn't possibly be hearing.

Everyone on campus already suspected that she was very shaky these days. Sharing what she'd heard . . . what she'd *thought* she'd heard . . . would get her nothing but a one-way trip to a padded room. Anyone she told would say it had to have been a dream.

Well, of *course* it had been a dream. Couldn't be anything else. Couldn't . . .

"I said, what's wrong?" LuAnn repeated.

Katie dropped the comforter and slid to the edge of the bed. "Nothing!" she answered. "Not a thing. I was just thinking, that's all." It had to have been a dream. She'd only *thought* she was awake. Silly girl.

But . . . it had sounded as if Brownie was right there in the room with her. She could have sworn . . .

Shaking her head to clear it, Katie got up.

Twenty minutes later, she was frantically searching through the chaos of their room. "I left it right *here*!" she cried in frustration as LuAnn emerged from the bathroom. "I know I did!"

"Left what where?" LuAnn fastened tiny

pearl studs in her ears. "And how could you possibly hope to find anything in all this mess?"

"My sample budget for sociology class is missing. It was right here . . . somewhere."

"A budget? *You* worked up a budget?" LuAnn laughed. "That must have been a challenge. You've been spending lately as if you have your own money tree out on the Commons."

"It *was* a challenge!" Katie snapped. She crouched to rummage through a pile of clothing on the floor. "But I *did* it. And I need it *now*. It's due this afternoon. I *know* I finished it." She stood up, glancing around the room uncertainly. "I'm . . . I'm sure I did."

"Well, *I* never saw you working on it," LuAnn said, picking up her books. "I don't know when you would have done it. You're never here."

"I didn't do it here." She often went down to the river between classes and sat on the riverbank while she worked. But she hadn't shared that fact with anyone, especially LuAnn, who would call it "morbid." "I did it at the library."

"Well, happy hunting!" LuAnn walked to the door and opened it. "And since you're searching the room, maybe you could just . . . pick up a few things while you're at it? I'm too embarrassed to invite anyone in." Having said that, she left.

Katie didn't pick up a single thing. Her life was in chaos, why not her room? Before . . . before, she had believed that being neat and punctual and responsible, doing all the "proper" things, would keep terrible things from happening. If you were doing things the right way, wasn't your life supposed to turn out okay?

Wrong!

So, what was the point?

Katie didn't find her sample budget.

Campus was drenched in late-autumn sunshine. A gorgeous day . . . the stone and brick buildings standing tall, the leaves on the huge old trees scattered across the Commons blazing brilliant autumn colors of red and orange and gold. People hurried from building to building across the rolling lawns, carrying books and jackets. Everything looked so normal, so calm, so routine. . . .

It had *been* a dream. Had to be . . .

She ran into Davis out on the Commons. Although he claimed he was still half-asleep, he looked rested and healthy. She knew *she* didn't. For a brief moment, she was tempted to share her nightmare with him. Maybe if she shared it, it would fade more quickly.

But Davis had been Brownie's best friend. Telling him would bring back that look he'd had in his eyes when she'd returned to campus after two weeks away. That bleak look, his dark eyes sad and haunted. No, she couldn't tell Davis about her bad dream.

He walked her to class. They talked about ordinary things . . . assignments, lunch in the dining hall at the Quad, an upcoming dance. They were both very careful to avoid any mention of Brownie.

She couldn't get used to that. He had been such a big part of their lives — one of the best parts, and yet now they never talked about him. It was almost as if he'd never existed. That seemed so awful, so very wrong.

Maybe the others talked about him when she wasn't around. Maybe, although they all denied it, they really did blame her. Maybe they secretly agreed with what Brownie's voice had accused the night before: that it was her fault. And so they didn't talk about him in front of her because they were afraid they'd reveal how they honestly felt.

But . . . it's *not* my fault, she told herself, it's *not*. Everyone said it wasn't. . . .

Until last night.

Her English lit professor had to call on her three times before she responded, and when she got to psych class, she discovered that she was unprepared. There had been an assignment . . . she hadn't heard it being assigned, hadn't written it in her notebook, hadn't done it.

Her professor was not happy with her.

"Your grade is rapidly dwindling from a healthy B to a questionable C," he told her after class. He did not smile at her. "I do not tolerate slackers, Ms. Sullivan. I hadn't pegged you as one. Was that a mistake on my part?"

She mumbled some sort of promise, and escaped.

This wasn't the first time she'd been reprimanded by one of her teachers. She'd tried . . . she'd tried so hard since she came back. That budget . . . she was positive she had finished it. Where *was* it? It was so hard to concentrate. It took every ounce of concentration she had just to keep from seeing Brownie being swept away in that wild, angry river. There wasn't much concentration left for anything else.

She would have to try harder.

It seemed stupid to go to sociology class without her assignment. So instead, Katie volunteered to drive her friends to the mall. Only Allen objected, telling Katie she couldn't afford to cut again.

"I'll get the notes from someone," she said airily, and started the car.

Tried to start the car.

It sputtered, chugged, sputtered again, and died.

"Oh, great!" Katie wailed. "Just great! Like I really need *this* today? What's wrong with it?"

"Nothing," Allen said. He was sitting beside her in the front seat. "Look at your gas gauge."

Katie looked. And groaned. The needle was on the wrong side of EMPTY.

"C'mon guys," Allen said to Davis, LuAnn, and Callie in the backseat, "it's the shuttle or walking. This girl forgot to fill her tank."

"No! No, I didn't." Katie remained behind the wheel, staring at the gauge. "I had it filled Saturday. And I haven't even driven it that much. It *couldn't* be empty." She reached out and tapped the glass covering the gauge.

The needle didn't budge.

"This is nuts," she said slowly, thoughtfully. "I *did* fill it up."

"Are you sure?" Davis asked, leaning over the front seat to study the gauge. "Maybe you meant to, and then forgot."

Oh, great. First LuAnn hints that a missing assignment is a figment of Katie's imagination, and now Davis is practically accusing her of total brain drain.

"Don't you think I *know* when my gas tank is being filled? I filled it myself, for pete's sake!"

"You *never* use self-service," Allen said.

"I never used to," she said. "*Past* tense. I do now. And I *know* I filled the tank last Saturday. It couldn't possibly be empty."

"Well, it *is*," Allen retorted. "Give it up. We'll bring a can of gas back from that station near the mall."

"Maybe you have a leak," Callie said placatingly as they all climbed out of the car.

"Well, if I do, it's a very *big* leak," Katie said irritably. She didn't believe for a second that she had a gasoline leak. She had had the Honda thoroughly checked out before she'd taken it to school.

Then what *had* happened to nearly ten dollars worth of gas?

I've had worse days, Katie reminded herself as they all climbed aboard the crowded yellow shuttle bus into town. I've had days that make today look like a picnic in the park.

It didn't get any better.

When they had eaten their pizza in the mall's food court, and it was time to pay, Katie reached into her purse for her wallet.

It wasn't there.

But . . . she had put it in there herself. Yesterday, when she'd switched from her brown purse to her black one. And she hadn't removed it since.

"*Now* what are you hunting for?" LuAnn asked, watching Katie searching in vain through the fat shoulderbag.

Did she have to say it like that? As if Katie Sullivan couldn't find her own face in a mirror?

"Nothing," she said, removing her hand from her purse. She was *not* going to admit she'd . . . misplaced something. Again. "I just left my money in my other purse. Or," glaring pointedly at Davis, "maybe I spent it all on gas last Saturday."

Davis just laughed.

On the way home, Katie sat staring out the shuttle window, glumly going over the day's puzzles.

She came up with no satisfactory answers to any of her questions.

When they reached Nightingale Hall, LuAnn decided to get off, and urged Katie to come with her. "We're going to talk about Linda's birthday party. I'm helping with it. Maybe you could help, too?"

The last thing in the world Katie felt like doing was walking up that gravel driveway and into that gloomy old brick house. Well . . .

maybe not the *last* thing. Next-to-last. A house, even a creepy one, full of people, had to be better than an empty dorm room right now.

Davis, Allen, and Callie decided to come along. Together, they all trudged up the hill.

Chapter 8

When they reached the top of the hill, the house seemed less ominous.

Katie's eyes were drawn to the old metal fire escape on the left side of the house. Rusted in spots, it led from the ground all the way up beyond the third floor to a small window below the roofline. The window was open.

Attic, she thought to herself. She loved attics. They always smelled so . . . well, so attic-y. Stale and musty and of cedar and mothballs.

"Neat fire escape," she commented, automatically moving toward it. Up there in that attic, she'd bet, was utter, total peace and quiet. A place to rest. She really needed to rest.

"Where are you going?" Allen called as Katie quickened her steps.

"Think that rusty old thing will hold me?" She called over her shoulder. "Looks like it would be really fun to climb. I think I'll try it out."

Allen groaned. Davis laughed, and Callie and LuAnn exchanged a glance that said, She *wouldn't* . . . *would* she?

"You *hate* heights!" Allen called. "Remember?"

"Used to," Katie replied. *"Used to!"* She kept advancing toward the fire escape. "Someone needs to check this thing out, make sure it's in good working order. There's a window open on the second floor. I don't see a screen. I'll go in the house that way. Meet you all inside, okay?"

It was, they all knew, exactly the sort of thing Brownie would have done.

"Are you *nuts*?" Allen shouted, his face red with anger. "That thing looks like it might collapse if a *leaf* fell on it. Will you cut it *out*? This isn't funny."

Katie shrugged and kept going, her steps light but purposeful.

"If you're determined to kill yourself," Allen continued, "don't expect me to stay here and watch you do it!" He hesitated for a moment, hoping Katie would change her mind. When she didn't, he turned in disgust and began walking rapidly toward the house.

LuAnn followed.

Davis and Callie waited at the foot of the fire escape.

"C'mon up!" Katie called down when she reached the first set of windows. She could see people inside, in a large room. She was already feeling dizzy from the height, and had to grip the narrow railing tightly. But she grinned down at Davis and Callie. "What's the matter?" she teased. "Are you guys chicken? It's great up here!"

"Not chicken!" Callie retorted. "Just sane! See you inside."

When it became clear to Davis that Katie wasn't going to change her mind, he, too, went inside.

When Katie reached the second floor window, she hesitated. The window *was* open. All she had to do was climb inside.

But . . . there was still that smaller window open two floors above her. She'd have to go awfully high . . . almost to the roof.

It was tempting. She'd already come this far. It would be quiet up there. If she went up there instead of joining everyone else, she wouldn't have to listen to a lecture from Allen, wouldn't have to feel the curious eyes of Nightmare Hall's residents on her. They'd be wondering why she'd been climbing around on the fire escape, and if she really was losing it.

She didn't feel like dealing with any of that.

She kept going, all the way up to the top window.

It was small, but so was she. She slid over the windowsill on her stomach. When she was standing, she breathed in the welcome attic smell, and glanced around.

It was stuffy inside. The ceiling sloped sharply on both sides, and the only light came from the little window. The corners of the large room were deeply shadowed.

Katie made her way cautiously around the room, careful not to bump into the trunks and suitcases, boxes and old furniture filling the space. She couldn't see very well, and felt with her hands along the walls. When she encountered a doorknob in a side wall under the eaves, she turned the knob.

The door opened into a long, narrow closet filled with large white plastic garment bags, suspended from a thick metal rod. They were huge and fat, and looked like refrigerators. The ceiling was low, and the bottoms of the bags rested on the floor.

A light string brushed her shoulder. She yanked on it, and a pale yellow light filled the closet.

Curious, she began opening the fat, heavy plastic bags and inspecting the contents. Beautiful antique clothing . . . wedding gowns, dresses, shawls, coats.

"Maybe I could borrow something for Halloween," Katie murmured, fingering the smooth, shiny fabric of a severe-looking, floor-length, long-sleeved gown of navy blue. A bouquet of faded artificial violets was fastened to the yellowing lace collar. It was the only garment hanging in the third bag.

Lost in what she was discovering, Katie completely forgot where she was.

That was a mistake.

Because when she accidentally scratched her finger on something sharp near the collar of the navy dress, she instinctively jerked upright in pain . . .

And the back of her head cracked against something hard and unyielding.

The pain and force of the blow sent her to her knees. She managed only a small, soft moan before everything turned dark and she fell forward, her eyes shutting.

When she awoke, it took her several painful minutes to become aware of three things. One, her head felt as if it had been split in two by an axe. Two, she didn't have enough air. She was having trouble breathing. And three, she was almost entirely surrounded by white. It was above her, below her, and all around her.

Was she in a hospital?

No . . . she wasn't lying in a hospital bed. She seemed to be crumpled up in a ball in the white enclosure . . . lying on . . . the floor? But not the *bare* floor. There was white underneath her, too.

Katie struggled to sit up, groaning when her injured head throbbed in protest. She reached out hesitantly and jabbed a finger into the white on one side. It was pliable but strong. Plastic . . . she was sitting at the bottom of a tall column of white plastic, like a long white box standing on end.

A box . . . like a refrigerator . . .

She turned toward the fourth side. Unlike the other three sides, this one seemed to be navy blue. It smelled old and stale and hung from the top of the box to the bottom. Looking upward, Katie saw that the navy blue belonged to the antique dress she'd been looking at before she hit her head. Its hanger was looped over a thin metal rod across the top of the enclosure.

And then she knew where she was. She couldn't believe it. She was *inside* the garment bag, the one she'd been looking into when she'd hit her head.

No . . . no, that was crazy. She *couldn't* be.

But . . . why not? The garment bag was taller

and wider than she was and the zipper ran not only down the front center, but also along the top, creating a flap when opened that resembled a tent door. That flap had been hanging wide open when she fell forward.

In spite of her aching head, Katie almost laughed aloud with relief. She had fallen into a garment bag?

She did laugh then. She couldn't help it.

She pushed the navy blue dress aside, joking, "Hope I didn't bruise you when I slammed into you," and then stared in shock at the place where the flap should have been hanging wide open, waiting for her to step out into the stuffy, cedar-y smell of the attic closet.

There was no opening.

The zippers were clearly there, tiny highways running down the middle and along the top of the fat white bag.

But . . . they . . . were . . . *closed*.

Chapter 9

Katie sat perfectly still, on the floor of the portable closet. So much white . . . it hurt her eyes.

The bag had been *unzipped* when she hit her head and everything went black. She could have fallen forward, into the open bag.

But she couldn't have zipped it *closed*. The zippers were on the *outside*. One ran up and down the center, the other across the top. Their tiny little teeth were fastened solidly together, like a child balking at a spoonful of spinach.

Someone . . . someone had zipped her in?

No . . . no . . .

But the bag *was* zipped. Closed. To keep out moths and damaging light and . . . to keep *her* inside.

She had to get out of here. There wasn't enough air.

She raised herself to her knees. Running fingers along the zipper path, she searched for a way to open the heavy plastic bag.

There was nothing. No flopping little metal lever on the zippers. Nothing to grab and pull.

Because the manufacturer hadn't seen a need for it. He hadn't expected someone to be *inside* his portable closet. It had been designed for clothes. And how much air did clothes need?

This was *not* funny. She was kneeling inside a heavy plastic bag that was closed from the outside.

Still, it *was* plastic . . . not steel or wood. She could probably punch a hole in it, couldn't she?

She tried. She poked, gently at first, then harder. The plastic bounced back into place each time. Then she hit out harder, grunting with the effort. And kicked, wishing she were wearing pointed heels instead of flats. But the thick white plastic seemed impenetrable.

The feeling of being closed in was getting to her. Because she was small and the garment bag wasn't, she had some room to maneuver. But all that white around her . . . above her, below her, so close to her on all sides, hurt her head. And the realization that getting out was not going to be a simple matter, as she'd first thought, was creating a swell of panic within her.

Of course she would get out. . . . of course
. . . but . . . how?

Then, as the idea hit her that she might *not*
get out, she panicked. She began beating
against the walls of the bag with both fists, and
kicking out with her feet. "You're just *plastic*!"
she shouted, pounding and kicking, "you're just
plastic! You can't *keep* me in here!"

But her efforts were in vain. The white fabric
remained solid and unmoving.

Exhausted, she sank back on her haunches,
shaking.

After a few minutes, she forced herself to
breathe more evenly in an effort to calm down.
Then she ran her fingers along the zippers
again. One finger stung sharply as she continued doggedly to trace the zipper paths. A faint
trail of red followed it across the white plastic.

She remembered, then, why she had jerked
backward and hit her head. She'd been exam-
ining the navy blue dress, fingering the lace
collar and had ripped her finger open on something sharp. It had hurt. . . .

Something sharp . . .

Katie reached up to yank the navy blue gown
from its hanger. When it was lying in her lap,
she could see tiny spots of bright red on the
yellowing collar.

She carefully lifted its edges, and probed gingerly around the bouquet of artificial violets.

There . . . right there! A large, wicked-looking pin . . . a hatpin. The kind her grandmother used. It was holding the fake corsage in place.

Maybe . . .

Katie carefully unfastened the flowers.

The pin was sharply pointed, and seemed strong, unbending in her hand.

Her head ached, and her chest hurt. Air . . . she needed air. Even the musty, stale attic air would be better than this airless white tomb.

Dizzy with the need for oxygen, she poked the sharp point into the heavy white plastic, beside the zipper.

The plastic resisted, and the hatpin bounced backward.

Katie bit down hard on her lower lip. This was no cheap two-dollar garment bag. This was hurricane-and-flood-proof plastic. But the hatpin *had* to work. It *had* to! She had nothing else with her. No purse, no sharp objects in her jeans pockets, no nail file or sharp-edged keys. Nothing. The nasty-looking hatpin was her only hope.

Even if someone came all the way up to the attic looking for her, they might not come into the closet. And screaming for help would take up too much oxygen. Not that anyone on the lower floors would *hear* her, no matter how loud she yelled. When she arrived in the attic, she'd heard at least three stereos competing with one another on the lower floors.

Drawing her right arm backward as far as she could in her limited space, Katie thrust the hatpin forward into the plastic with all her strength.

It penetrated, making a small hole.

But when she tried to pull it back out again, she couldn't.

It was stuck.

That tiny little hole did her no good at all. It wasn't even large enough to peek out.

She had to twist and pull and yank on the hatpin's oval pearl tip until her shoulders ached. Finally, just as she was about to give up, it made a sudden little popping sound and hiccoughed backward, out of the plastic.

She was almost afraid to try again. If the hatpin stuck a second time, she didn't think she would have the strength to wrestle with it.

But what choice did she have? She was running out of air, and that teeny little hole wouldn't let in enough to keep a flea alive.

This time she drew the pin backwards and stabbed the plastic at an angle, hoping the sharp point would be driven downward as it penetrated.

It was.

With a faint ripping sound, the hatpin stabbed the white plastic and continued sliding downward, splitting the cover as it went.

The resulting tear was only a thin slit down the center of the bag. But it was all Katie needed. She was able to slide her hand through the slit, fumble around for the zipper tag, and, when she found it, yank on it to pull it down, an inch or two at a time.

Finally, she had a large enough space to crawl through.

Gasping with relief, she tumbled forward through the opening, onto the closet floor.

The temptation to remain there was strong. She was so sleepy, and her head hurt. It felt better when she kept her eyes closed.

But the air in the closet wasn't much better than inside the garment bag. She couldn't stay where she was.

Katie opened her eyes.

It was dark. She had been so glad to be free of the bag, she hadn't even noticed, before she closed her eyes, that the light she had turned on when she entered the closet was no longer shining.

She couldn't see a thing.

Had the bulb burned out?

Or . . . had someone turned it off?

Afraid of the low-hanging beams, Katie crawled on her hands and knees to the nearest wall and felt along it for the door. She had left it open . . . but then, she'd left the light on, too, and now the closet was dark.

How had that happened? Who had closed the door?

Had they . . . her heart sank . . . had they *locked* the door, too? Did it *have* a lock on it? She couldn't remember.

Sweat gathered on her forehead and hands. Her head throbbed. If she didn't get out of this horrible place soon . . .

There! A hinge, a crease in the wood . . .

Katie raised up on her knees and felt for the doorknob. If it didn't turn . . .

It turned.

And a second later, she was lying in the big attic, the closet door open behind her.

No soothing breeze from an open window cooled her. It was almost as stifling as it had been in the closet.

She turned her head toward the window she'd entered.

It was closed. The small white lace curtains that had blown around her as she crawled in hung perfectly still.

Someone had definitely been up here.

When she had caught her breath, Katie sat

up. The room spun like a carousel. Sweat dripped into her lap. Tiny pink and purple spots danced before her eyes.

If I don't get up right *now*, she told herself, I won't . . . get up . . . at *all*.

She got up.

Walking unsteadily, Katie made her way across the attic, opened the door, and went downstairs. The air that brushed her face as she left the attic was cool, and steadied her.

Although Nightingale Hall's upper-story layout was unfamiliar, all she had to do was follow the staircase.

But she felt faint . . . couldn't make it all the way down, couldn't . . . was going to pass out at any moment . . . there! that open door . . . a bathroom . . . water . . .

She went inside, to put a cool wet cloth on her face. It helped. Then she sat on the edge of the tub long enough to pull herself together. She didn't want the others to see her red-faced and sweaty.

They would say it was her own fault, for being stupid enough to climb the fire escape in the first place.

When she felt almost normal again, she continued on down the stairs. Reaching the first floor, she followed the sound of voices to a large, high-ceilinged room with a fireplace. Her friends were sprawled on the oriental carpet or sitting on the overstuffed furniture, talking with tall, blonde Linda Carlyle.

Callie was the first to look up and see Katie leaning against the doorframe. "Katie! What are you doing back here?"

Katie moved into the room, her legs still shaky. "Back here? I never left. I . . . I was . . . trapped . . . up in the attic."

Callie laughed. Linda, Allen, and LuAnn joined in.

But Davis got up quickly and crossed the room to Katie's side. "You look a little weird. What happened?" He led her to a chair. When she was seated, she told them what had happened. She spoke haltingly, knowing how incredible her story must seem. She could hardly believe it herself . . . and she'd *been* there.

And she watched as LuAnn's cheeks turned red. She's embarrassed, Katie thought angrily. She thinks I've gone over the edge and she's embarrassed for me.

"If you don't believe me," she said coolly, "check the lump on the back of my head." When she reached up and gently touched the spot herself, her fingers came away wet with sticky red.

Callie gasped. Davis offered to call a doctor.

"No doctor," Katie said firmly. "It's not that bad. Just a cut and a bump."

Davis instead went in search of some ice and some antiseptic.

"We *did* hunt for you," Allen told Katie. "Looked all over the house. Not in the attic, though. No one thought you'd go up that high."

"When we didn't find you," Callie added, "we decided you'd changed your mind about the fire escape, like the sensible person you used to be, and gone back to campus."

Davis returned with the housemother, Mrs. Coates, a short, plump woman with graying hair. She examined Katie's wound, cleansed it with wet cotton balls, and applied antiseptic. She apologized several times, although she was clearly perplexed about what Katie had been doing in the attic.

"Exploring," Katie finally said. She saw no need to mention her climb up the fire escape, and hoped no one else would. "You have some beautiful old clothes up there. But I'm afraid I ruined one of those big white garment bags. The ones in the attic closet that look like refrigerators?"

"Oh, my friend Maddie brought those back from Hong Kong. Aren't they nice? This old house doesn't have much closet space, so they've really come in handy." She frowned. "You say you ruined one?"

Katie nodded. "I'll show you. I'll pay for it, of course. But it really wasn't my fault. Someone zipped it up after I hit my head and fell into the bag. I had to rip it to get out, or I would have suffocated."

Katie stood up, and swayed precariously. Davis grabbed her arm and supported her.

"I want all of you to come," Katie commanded. "When you see the bag, you'll quit looking at me like that."

"Like what?" LuAnn asked innocently. But she and the others dutifully followed Katie back up the flights of stairs to the attic.

"Someone was up here," Katie said as they entered the attic, "because that window was open when I went into the closet. And it wasn't when I came out."

"Oh, I closed it, dear," the housemother said. "I had it open to air things out up here. But I knew it would chill the house if I left it open after the sun went down."

"*You* were up here?"

"Yes. But I didn't see *you*. There wasn't anyone here when I closed the window."

"I was in the closet." Katie pointed. "I knocked myself out on one of those low beams. I must have been unconscious when you were up here. That's why you didn't hear anything. Was the closet door open and the light on?"

Mrs. Coates pursed her lips in concentration. "Oh, I don't *think* so. I would have noticed."

"Come on, I'll show you where it happened," Katie said, and led the way to the closet.

The light came on when she yanked on the string. So it wasn't burned out. But Mrs. Coates said *she* hadn't turned it off or closed the closet door.

Someone else had.

"It's right here," Katie said, yanking the first two portable closets forward. "I'm really sorry I had to make a hole, but I had no choice . . ." her voice broke off as she stared at the third bag. It was completely intact. The zippers were closed, and there wasn't so much as a nick in the white plastic.

"That's weird," she said slowly to the group bunched up in the doorway. "I know it was the third bag. The first one had the wedding dress in it, the second one had the gowns, and the navy blue dress was in the third bag, I'm positive. There was just that one dress. That's why there was room enough for me."

There was no hatpin slit in the fourth bag, either. Or the fifth.

And although she went back to the beginning

and started over, checking each bag thoroughly, she found nothing.

Moving faster now, she went through the same routine three more times, her eyes darting from the top of each bag to the bottom, and from side to side.

Not a single bag had been damaged in any way.

Chapter 10

Katie could feel skeptical eyes on her. That made her mad. If they knew what she'd just gone through . . .

She examined each bag again, slowly, taking her time, going over them with her eyes, sliding her hand down the front to feel for a narrow slit.

There was no hatpin rip in any of the bags.

Katie lifted her head. "Mrs. Coates," she asked, "how many of these bags did your friend give you?"

"Why, I don't really know," the housemother answered. "She brought them to the house, showed them to me, and then she and one of the students living here brought them up and put my antique clothes in them."

"You weren't with them?"

"No. I'd fallen a few weeks earlier and couldn't manage the stairs."

Great. Katie knew one of the big white bags had to be missing. But without Mrs. Coates's help, how could she prove it?

She left Nightmare Hall shaken and frustrated. Someone had tried to suffocate her up in the attic. There was no other explanation for what had happened.

But she was the only one who believed that, which made for a very lonely feeling.

It wasn't that they weren't kind. They were sorry, all very sorry, that she'd been trapped in the attic, sorry she'd hit her head, sorry she was upset. Callie said it must have been very scary inside all that white plastic, and LuAnn, her blue eyes wide, said, "It's a good thing you found that hatpin," and Davis nodded solemnly. And Allen told a story about a friend of his in third grade who had crawled into an abandoned refrigerator on someone's back porch, and nearly died. "Same kind of thing," he said sympathetically, holding Katie's hand. "Not enough air. Good thing someone found him in time."

But no one said, "We have to find out who did this to you, Katie." Which was what she needed to hear.

When they got back to the Quad, she told LuAnn she was going downstairs to get a soda from the vending machine.

"Don't you think you should be checked out at the infirmary?" LuAnn said. "You still look awfully flushed from being stuck in that attic, Katie. Davis told me on the way home that he thought you should see a doctor."

What *kind* of doctor? Katie thought cynically. A shrink? Aloud, she said, "I'm fine. Just thirsty, that's all. Be right back."

But she didn't come right back. Because she'd never intended to go downstairs for a Coke. Instead, she went to the river. She needed to think.

Dusk was falling. It would be dark soon. She'd never minded walking along the river in the dark. She knew the path behind campus by heart. It ran side-by-side with the river, with a few twists and turns that she had traveled many times. Her feet had moved swiftly and surely.

But it was different now, being outside, alone, when darkness was on its way. Whatever anyone else thought, someone *had* stuffed her into that garment bag and zipped it closed. Someone had tried to kill her. So being outside, behind campus, with darkness falling, wasn't the same as it had been. Everywhere she went now, she would have to look over her shoulder, be careful who she talked to, keep her eyes open for anything that seemed threatening.

How did you know what was threatening and what wasn't? She hadn't thought she'd be in danger in the attic at Nightmare Hall. But . . . she'd been wrong.

Still, she kept going. She needed to think. She did that best in her favorite spot, on the riverbank halfway between the canoe landing, and the ugly black railroad bridge, old and useless now.

No one was jogging or hiking along the path. Maybe she was safe here. If anyone did come by, the bushes along the path would keep her hidden.

Relieved to be away from the concerned eyes of her friends, Katie sat on a low, flat rock beside the river. The water level had gone down considerably recently, and although it was still muddy, it was much quieter, a lazy ribbon ambling along, taking its time . . .

If Brownie had fallen into the river when it was like this, he'd be sitting beside her now.

Tears stinging her eyelids, Katie slipped her shoes and socks off and dug her bare toes into the mud at the edge of the water. It felt cool and soothing as it squooshed between her toes.

GUILTY, someone had written on her car. GUILTY.

Was she guilty? If she hadn't panicked that day . . .

It didn't matter what *she* thought. Someone *else* thought so. Didn't it look like someone had judged her guilty and was now trying to punish her? Or was she being totally paranoid?

No. Not paranoid. It seemed frighteningly clear that someone was very angry with her. She could have died in that portable closet at Nightmare Hall. If it hadn't been for the hatpin, she wouldn't be sitting on this grassy riverbank now, breathing plenty of fresh, cool air and feeling soft, wet mud between her toes.

"I don't know why you're afraid of the river," he said as she hesitated at the edge of the canoe. *"Didn't your father ever take you fishing?"*

"No. He took me to the ballet. It was perfectly safe at the ballet."

"It's safe on the river. I know how to handle a canoe. Don't you trust me?"

"It's not you I don't trust. It's this wild and crazy river."

And she'd been right, hadn't she? If only she'd stuck to her guns, just once, instead of doing what Brownie wanted. . . .

Her right foot poked into a patch of drier dirt. It crumbled around her toes, creating a small tunnel. Her toes explored, and bumped into something firmer than mud. An object . . . small, square.

Katie pulled it out with her toes. Curious,

she reached down to pick it up and wiped the excess dirt off on the grass.

A wallet . . . a brown leather wallet.

She opened it.

There was barely enough daylight left to see by. But there was enough to see the brown curly hair and laughing dark eyes that looked back at her from a driver's license photo encased in plastic.

Katie's breath caught in her throat. The name on the license jumped out at her.

BROWN, ROBERT XAVIER.

Katie closed the wallet, crying quietly.

His . . . it was *his*.

It must have been lying hidden in the riverbank all this time. Buried. Ripped from his pocket by the river and driven into the mud along the riverbank.

Callie . . . Callie should have it. Brownie's parents would want it.

She would give the wallet to Callie.

But first . . .

Wiping her tears with one muddy hand, Katie opened the wallet again.

She forced herself to study the picture on the license. Brownie was the only person she'd ever known who had a grin in his eyes. It was always there, even in a tacky driver's license photo.

There were other pictures, plastic-covered. Katie thumbed through them. Brownie standing in front of his car, probably taken on the day he bought it. Brownie and Callie together, wearing silly party hats. Someone's birthday. Callie's high school yearbook picture. She looked beautiful.

There was a fourth plastic sleeve, but it was empty.

Disappointment flooded Katie. That sleeve, she remembered, had held a picture of her and Brownie that Callie had taken at a campus tennis match. Brownie and Callie had won at doubles. They had all celebrated afterward with a picnic at the state park.

Katie loved that picture. She and Brownie were looking at each other instead of staring straight into the camera. They were both smiling.

Brownie had loved it, too. It was he who had taken the negatives to the mall and ordered two wallet-sized photos. "So we can carry it with us all the time," he'd said. He'd put one in his wallet and given her the other one. She had loved the idea of just the two of them having copies of the picture. Something they alone shared.

It seemed terribly unfair that of all the pictures in his wet and muddy wallet, only that one had been ripped free by the river.

Katie felt incredibly sad as she got up and, carrying her shoes and socks in one hand, the wallet in the other, returned to the dorm. All the way back, she checked constantly to make sure no one was following her or approaching from the side.

No one was.

"Where have you been?" LuAnn shrieked when Katie walked into their room. "You were gone forever! I looked all over for you . . . Katie, you look terrible. Your face is all dirty. Where *were* you?"

"At the river." Katie sank down on her bed. "I . . . I found Brownie's wallet."

LuAnn's face paled. "The river? His wallet? Katie, you shouldn't go there. It's not healthy. It'll make you. . . ." LuAnn hesitated.

Katie lifted her head. "Crazy? Is that what you were going to say?"

LuAnn's face went from white to red.

"I know that's what you're all thinking, LuAnn. But someone *did* zip me into one of those portable closets and I *did* use a hatpin to get out, whether you believe it or not. Here," she added, extending the wallet toward LuAnn, "give this to Davis tomorrow. He's in your math class, right? Tell him to give it to Callie."

LuAnn recoiled as if the wallet were on fire. "No! *You* give it to him. Anyway, he and Callie aren't an item anymore."

"They're not?"

"Mm-mm. They don't hate each other or anything like that. They're just not dating anymore."

"Is Callie upset?"

LuAnn shrugged. "Doesn't seem to be. Anyway, *you* give her the wallet. You're the one who found it."

She'd give it to Callie, not to Davis. He thought she was crazy, thought she needed to see a doctor.

So she was surprised the next morning, after LuAnn had left for class, when Davis showed up at her door, wanting to know if she'd like to go downstairs to the Quad caf for coffee.

"Have you ever *had* coffee downstairs?" Katie asked to cover her surprise.

"Yeah. It was awful. But I've got a nine o'clock, so time is of the essence. The coffee may be rivermud, but it's right here at hand. Okay with you?"

As long as you don't look at me as if I might jump up and start dancing on one of the tables at any second, Katie thought. Aloud, she said, "Sure. Might get me jump-started."

"Didn't sleep much?" he asked sympathetically as they left the room.

She didn't want sympathy. She wanted someone to understand that she was telling the truth about everything that had happened. "I slept fine," she said coolly.

He was decent enough not to say, "You're lying."

In the busy Quad caf, they ate bagels and drank the horrible coffee and talked about trivial things. They were surrounded by sleepy-eyed students who couldn't even comb their hair until they'd had coffee. A few scribbled frantically, putting the finishing touches on assignments as they sipped. Most stared off into space, unwilling to face the day just yet.

Finally, Davis cleared his throat and said, "Katie. . . . I think maybe you should check out one of the campus doctors."

She set her coffee mug down hard on the table. "Doctors? Davis, why don't you just spit it out? You mean shrink, right?"

"Look," he said, leaning across the table toward her, "you've been through hell lately. Everyone knows it, and everyone understands."

Well, no, not really. They didn't understand at all.

"But you're trying to handle everything by yourself, and that's not good."

No kidding.

"You never even *talk* about Brownie," Davis continued. "None of us do. We don't want to upset you. It doesn't seem to take much these days. You should be talking to someone about what happened."

Katie wasn't listening. She was thinking that Davis had a very nice face. Not as full of laughter as Brownie's, but the same dark hair, only straighter, longer, and with a hint of red in it. Dark eyes, too, but without the constant grin. The eyes were very serious now, as Davis went on and on about how she needed help.

Well, yes, she did need that. But not the kind Davis was suggesting. What she needed was to be taken seriously. How could she get the help she needed if no one believed that someone was out to punish her?

"I would love to talk about Brownie," she said finally. "But no one wants to. Too depressing. I guess it's easier for people to pretend he's just away on vacation or something."

"Well, if it's too painful for his friends to talk about him, then please, find someone else to talk to. It's important, Katie."

She lifted her head to look straight at him. "Did Allen send you here? To talk to me?"

Davis looked honestly puzzled. "Allen? No, why?"

She shrugged. "It's the kind of thing he would do. Seems to think he has to look out for me. I keep telling him he doesn't, but . . ."

"He's worried about you," Davis said seriously. "We all are."

Then why didn't they *help* her? Why didn't they believe her? Okay, so she'd fallen apart that day at the river, screaming, crying, unwilling to leave. She'd had to be dragged away by the police. And then she'd had to leave campus. But she was back, wasn't she? And since she'd returned, she hadn't done anything crazier than the things Brownie had done. But they'd never accused *him* of being crazy.

Still, she told Davis politely that she would think about what he'd said, hoping that would make him back off. To show him how "normal" she was, she told him jokingly that she didn't really think she could thank him for the coffee, since it tasted like sludge. Then, keeping a friendly smile pasted across her face, Katie picked up her books and left the dining hall.

She managed to keep the smile on most of the day. She went to her classes, paid attention, took notes, had lunch with Allen and Callie at Vinnie's, their favorite off-campus pizza hangout. She did all the things that "normal" people were supposed to do. But she was very careful to keep other people around her all the time, just in case. And she didn't give Brownie's wallet to Callie.

She wasn't sure why. It was in her backpack. She'd brought it with her for the express purpose of handing it over to Callie.

But Callie would get upset. And I would, too, Katie thought in dismay. Then we'd both start crying, right there in Vinnie's, and everyone would stare and point and whisper. And then her "normal" day, designed to show everyone that she wasn't falling totally apart, would be destroyed.

I'll give it to her later, Katie decided. She doesn't even know I have it, so there's no rush.

Watching Allen and Callie talking and joking together, she began to wonder if they wouldn't make a good couple, now that Callie and Davis were through. Katie would love to see Allen with someone as nice and funny as Callie. Besides, if Allen was romantically involved, he wouldn't have time to act like her keeper.

An uneasy feeling swept over her. Maybe this wasn't such a great time to be telling herself she didn't need a keeper, after what had happened the day before. It was really hard, thinking that someone out there hated you. It was hard keeping your eyes open every single second, watching for anyone who looked suspicious. She didn't even know what "suspicious" meant, exactly. What was it that she was supposed to be watching out for?

She didn't know.

She worked in the library for several hours that afternoon, then went home and took a nap. It was dark when she woke up. LuAnn and Linda were sitting on LuAnn's bed, studying. They looked up as Katie stirred. She hated the look in their eyes. Sympathy, for poor Katie, a basket case who had to sleep during the day just to stay afloat.

Well, she was *no* basket case. "Listen," she said when she was thoroughly awake, "you guys are on the swim team. How about we take a dip in that gorgeous, Olympic-sized pool?"

LuAnn laughed. "Katie, we can't do that. No one's there now."

Katie sat up. "Exactly! It'll be great! Come on! What's the use of having friends in high places if they can't do you any good?" And people were safe in threes. She wouldn't have to worry, with Linda and LuAnn along.

"We'll get in trouble," Linda pointed out.

"Only if we get caught. Can you get us in or not?"

"Well, sure," LuAnn answered reluctantly. "I mean, we can't get into the locker rooms.

But if we put our suits on here, under our clothes . . ."

"Well, come on, then!" Katie cried, jumping up and running over to her dresser to grab a swimsuit. "A dip is exactly what we all need." She hadn't been swimming since . . .

Well, it was time she got back into the water.

"If we get caught . . ." Linda said one more time.

"We *won't* get caught," Katie insisted. "And if we do, you can tell them it was all my fault." She laughed, a brittle sound. "Everyone knows I'm crazy!"

Five minutes later, the three left the room and headed for the Robeson Athletic Center.

Chapter 11

The water in the Olympic-sized pool felt wonderful. Cool and soothing, it unlocked Katie's muscles for the first time in many weeks. She wanted to stay in the water forever.

They didn't dare turn on any lights, so they swam in the dark. LuAnn and Linda spent so much time in the pool as members of the swim team, they didn't need to see. And Katie found the darkness comforting rather than scary. So quiet, so peaceful, the water drained tension and worries away from her. She could almost see all of it sliding away from her, down, down, through the deep waters of the pool, and out through the drain, to oblivion.

After an hour or so, LuAnn and Linda climbed out, saying they were starving.

Katie couldn't bear to leave. She was so relaxed, she felt she could have fallen asleep in the water. "If I had a life jacket on," she joked,

"I could probably get a decent night's sleep for a change. You two go ahead. I'll catch up. Just a few more minutes . . ."

LuAnn hesitated. "Katie, I don't think . . ."

"What?"

"Well, no one's supposed to be in the pool alone. It's a rule."

Katie laughed. "LuAnn, we're not supposed to be in here in the first place. Isn't it kind of late to be worried about rules?" Wondering if LuAnn had finally decided that Katie had been telling the truth about the attack in the attic she added, "I'm perfectly safe. Look, there's no one else here. So go on, give me some peace and quiet, okay? I *said* I'll catch up with you."

Realizing that she wasn't going to change her mind, the two girls left.

It was even better when they'd gone. So quiet, so peaceful. Katie could almost believe that she'd never seen that ugly word on her car, hadn't heard Brownie's voice telling her it was "all her fault." Her gas tank hadn't mysteriously emptied itself, and she hadn't been locked in a big white plastic garment bag. She could *almost* believe that it had all been just a bad dream.

Almost . . . but not quite.

Allen had checked her car over carefully. He'd found no sign of a gasoline leak.

But then, she hadn't expected him to.

Someone had deliberately drained her gas tank.

Allen said it was probably some guy with a hot date and no money for gas.

Maybe. Maybe not . . .

Still, floating on her back in the dark and silent pool, Katie could almost convince herself that *this* was reality. This peaceful, quiet bliss of floating in a pool of cool, placid water.

And if it *wasn't* reality, it *should* be.

When she heard a faint splash at the far end of the pool, she thought that LuAnn, worried about her, had returned to fetch her.

I'm *not* leaving until I'm good and ready! Katie thought defiantly.

But she stopped floating, treading water instead, and peered through the darkness for a sign of her roommate. "LuAnn? Is that you?"

A faint swishing sound met her ears. LuAnn was swimming toward her underwater? To surprise her? Scare her?

No. With LuAnn convinced that Katie was only one step away from completely losing her grip, she would never take a chance on pushing her that one extra step by scaring her half to death in a dark, empty pool.

Katie's heart stopped.

Someone *else* was in the water.

Chapter 12

Before Katie could take a deep breath and begin stroking her way to the edge of the pool, strong, cold hands grabbed both her ankles and yanked her beneath the surface of the water. The shock of being abruptly yanked beneath the surface paralyzed her briefly. Then panic set in. Someone was trying to *drown* her! She began struggling, fighting to kick free of the viselike grip around her ankles. Her arms flailed upward, reaching instinctively toward the surface . . . and *air*.

Suddenly, the grip on her ankles eased. But before she could dart to freedom, the same iron grip grabbed at her waist, snatching her downward again.

But . . . her feet were free.

She kicked out wildly, fiercely, aiming backward with quick, short jabs.

She connected. The heel of her left foot

slammed into something soft, and the grip around her waist relaxed.

She flew to the surface. *Get away, get away, have to get away.* . . .

Coughing, gasping for air, she had only enough time to fill her lungs with precious air before grasping hands clawed at her again, tugging her back into the water.

Her attacker was strong, with arms like steel.

Going to drown . . . drown . . . like Brownie . . . No, no!

Kicking was her only defense. She had to use her hands and arms to thrust upward, but she used her feet and legs like weapons. Each time her foot connected, the grip around her waist or shoulders eased and she darted to the surface to gulp in huge swallows of air.

And each time, before she could stroke to freedom, cruel hands grabbed her and dragged her down again.

Can't breathe, can't breathe . . . so dark down here, under the water . . . like a grave. . . .

The struggle seemed never-ending. She was tiring rapidly, her kicks becoming weaker. Her chest was on fire.

If only she could *see.* . . .

He was behind her, grabbing at her neck. Her left arm was free. . . .

Driven by terror and the desperate need for air, Katie bent her arm and drove her elbow backward in a short, vicious jab, praying it would hit something.

And almost screamed with pain as the elbow crashed into solid bone. A forehead? A jaw? Her arm went numb.

But then, suddenly, she was free, free to propel herself upward, free to swim, her left arm throbbing in agony. She raced to the edge of the pool and, exhausted, dragged her wet, tired body over the edge.

She lay on the cold tile only for a second. She dared take no longer.

It took every ounce of strength she had left to struggle to her feet and stumble away from the pool, to the door.

She never looked back.

But there wasn't a sound behind her. Not a sound. No splashing or thrashing in the water, no sign that anyone else had been in the pool with her.

But someone *had been*.

Had her elbow knocked him unconscious?

He could revive at any second and come after her.

No time to waste.

She had no towel, no clothes, no shoes. And

no time to stop and collect them. He meant to *kill* her.

Katie ran.

Racing down the long, narrow passageway outside the locker rooms, she wondered, Did Brownie suffer that way? Did he have that terrible pain in his chest, that horrible feeling of being suffocated by the water, that awful, desperate need for air?

The thought sickened her.

She ran around a corner and slammed, full force, into a security guard.

"What on earth . . . ?"

Katie, dripping wet and gasping for breath, backed away.

"Hey, what's going on here? You been in the pool? No one's supposed to be in the pool now. What'd you do, sneak in?" He was big and burly in his tan uniform, and he wasn't smiling.

Katie glanced back at the pool door. "Someone," she gasped, "someone tried to kill me! To drown me." She pointed toward the closed door. "In there."

"Kill you? Now, miss, that's no way to get out of being in trouble. Telling tall tales won't do it. I'm going to have to report you."

"Well, go ahead!" she shouted defiantly. She was cold and wet and scared. Her clothes were still back in the pool area, and she didn't even have a towel to warm her up. He could at least offer her his jacket. "But I'm telling you, someone just tried to *drown* me! He's still in there. I . . . I think I knocked him out with my elbow." She held up her arm for inspection. The elbow was red and beginning to swell.

The guard took no notice. "All right, miss, tell you what we'll do. Suppose you just show me where this attempted murderer is, and we'll have a little chat with him, okay?" He took her elbow, ignoring her painful wince, and led her back along the narrow passageway, aiming his flashlight in front of them.

When they got to the door, Katie hung back. "I don't want to go in there," she said quietly, shivering uncontrollably.

"Well, you did a few minutes ago," the guard said unsympathetically. "How am I supposed to find this perpetrator of yours if we don't go inside? You *did* say he was in there, didn't you?"

Jerk. But then, would *she* have believed someone who came racing out of the pool area in a bathing suit and screamed that someone had just tried to drown her?

I would *now*, she thought, and opened the pool door.

The flashlight illuminated the area around the pool. Katie saw her clothes, lying in a heap beside the tile trim, and ran to scoop them up. She threw them on over her sodden bathing suit as the guard played the light across the pool, from end to end and side to side.

There was no one in the water. No one swimming to safety, no one floating, unconscious. No one.

The guard shook his head. "Doesn't seem to be anyone here, miss. Now, could I have your name, please?"

Was there another exit from the pool? It was too dark to see. But there had to be. She couldn't believe it — her would-be executioner had slipped away, just when she'd thought she was finally going to learn his identity.

The guard took a small notebook from his shirt pocket. "What's your name, miss?"

"Jane Ellen McIver," Katie fibbed. "The Quad." She hoped there was no Jane Ellen McIver on campus. "Can you please give me a ride home? I'm cold."

"You haven't heard the last of this, Ms. McIver," he said. "We have rules, you know." But he gave her a ride in his little cart back to the dorm, and gave her only one more warning as he let her out. "You get caught breaking the rules," he said heartily, "it's always best to tell the truth."

"I'll remember that," she said, and, wrapping her arms around herself against the cool night air, hurried up the walkway into the dorm.

Her room was empty. She collapsed on her bed, not caring if she got the bedding wet, wanting only to be warm and safe. Her teeth chattered, and she was shaking so hard, the bed bumped against the wall.

She should call the police. Someone had tried to *kill* her. It hadn't been a joke or a game. It had been attempted *murder*. Or . . . attempted *execution*? Guilty, guilty. . . .

But she hadn't *seen* who was in the pool. And couldn't guess. And she had no proof that anything had happened, no proof at all. A bruised elbow? That wouldn't do it. If the security guard was any indication, people would be more interested in what she was doing in the pool than whether or not someone had tried to kill her.

The security guard hadn't believed her.

The police wouldn't, either.

Before she decided what to do, she *had* to get warm. A hot shower, dry clothes . . .

Maybe she'd be able to think better then.

When she came out of the shower, she noticed a note taped to the mirror. It told her that LuAnn had gone to Nightingale Hall to help with plans for Linda's birthday party the following night.

Any other time, Katie would have been happy to have the room all to herself. But not tonight. Someone on campus was very angry with her . . . even angrier now, probably . . . after she'd knocked him unconscious with her bony elbow.

Was he, even now, hunting for her?

Did he already know where she lived?

She was about to call LuAnn and ask her to come back, when a knock sounded at the door and Allen's voice called out, "Hey, anybody home?"

Relief flooded Katie. She ran to the door and yanked it open. And threw herself into Allen's arms. Davis was right behind him.

She immediately regretted her impulsive gesture. She drew back hastily. She didn't feel that way about Allen.

He looked very confused. "You okay?"

"What's wrong?" Davis asked.

She supposed it showed in her face. She was about to tell them what had happened when the phone rang. She ran over to answer it, leaving Allen and Davis in the doorway. . . .

. . . Where they couldn't see what *she* saw.

The call was for LuAnn. Katie took the message and hung up. But the entire time that she was speaking into the receiver, her eyes were fixed in disbelief on the silver picture frame standing on her bedside table.

That frame had been in the same spot, stationed amid the usual clutter of tissues and notebooks and pens, nail files and emery boards, jewelry and safety pins, for weeks. Katie hadn't touched it when she ran into the room in her bathing suit. Hadn't even glanced at it. Now, she couldn't believe her eyes.

"What's wrong?" Davis asked again, moving into the room.

Speechless, Katie pointed a shaking finger at the picture frame. Until now, it had housed a color photo of her parents, sitting in the backyard of their house in Rochester. They had been on their way to an awards dinner when the picture was taken. Her stepfather was wearing a tuxedo, her mother a beautiful black beaded gown, and they were smiling into the camera. Katie had always loved the photograph. Because she still missed her parents a little, she had given the picture a place of honor close to her bed.

"What?" Davis demanded, following Katie's pointing finger. "You're white as a ghost. The picture? What about it?"

And then she realized that of course he wouldn't understand. No wonder he looked puzzled. To him, and to Allen, it was just a picture in a frame.

What neither of them could know was, the picture in the frame wasn't the one she had put there.

Her parents were no longer smiling out at her.

Brownie was.

Chapter 13

"Why," Allen asked Katie, "are you staring at that picture as if you've never seen it before?"

"Because I *haven't*. It's not mine." Katie sat down on the bed, hands in her lap, her eyes glued to the picture frame. Brownie smiled back at her. She half-expected him to cry, "Surprise!"

Davis crouched beside Katie. "You didn't put that picture in there?"

"No." Katie regarded him soberly. "I had a picture of my parents in that frame. The only picture I have of Brownie is in my wallet." She didn't mention that that particular photograph was exactly like the one missing from Brownie's wallet.

Brownie's wallet . . . where *was* it? she suddenly wondered. She had intended to give it to Callie. . . . Where had she put it? Katie began searching the room for the wallet. It had to be here somewhere. . . .

She couldn't find it anywhere.

"What *are* you looking for?" Allen asked as Katie tossed aside books and papers and discarded clothing. "Not that you'd ever be able to find it in this mess."

"Never mind the housekeeping tips," she said. If they knew what she'd been through tonight . . . "I've lost my wallet. Help me look. It's brown leather, and kind of dirty. I dropped it in the mud the last time it rained."

"Your wallet is *red*," Allen reminded her, watching her run from one cluttered surface to another. "I gave it to you for your birthday last year, remember?"

She could have told them, then, that it was Brownie's wallet she was hunting for. But, remembering the looks they'd given her after the garment bag incident, she decided not to tell them yet that she'd found Brownie's wallet on the riverbank, until she could produce it. If she didn't have it to show them, they'd never believe her.

But she couldn't find it. It was gone.

Someone had come into her room, switched the pictures in the silver frame, and taken Brownie's wallet. They must have picked it up accidentally at first, because only LuAnn knew that Katie had it. Then, when they'd seen who it belonged to, they'd taken it.

Because this person believed she was to blame for Brownie's death.

Somehow, she had to prove she wasn't. But *how*?

Until she figured out a way to do that, she wasn't safe. Not safe at all . . .

Earlier, she had found her own wallet — the wallet that had been missing from her purse at the mall. She accidentally discovered it lying inside a notebook. She knew she hadn't put it there. Someone else had.

That seemed unimportant now, except to emphasize the fact that she wasn't safe even in her own room. Someone had been there. And might come back . . .

She knew, without being told, that both Davis and Allen suspected that she had switched the pictures herself and forgotten that she'd done it. Like failing to fill her gas tank and losing her assignment. That made her so mad, she decided not to tell them about the incident in the pool. Let them think she was pale and shaky because she hadn't been sleeping. Let them think she was falling apart. She didn't care what they thought. If they weren't going to believe her. . . .

"Did you tell anyone I had Brownie's wallet?" were the first words out of Katie's mouth when LuAnn walked into the room half an hour later. She had sent Davis and Allen home because while she was tearing the place apart searching for Brownie's wallet, they'd both been looking at her as if they expected her to take wing and start flying around the room at any second. Better to be alone and scared than to feel like she was setting her friends' teeth on edge.

Allen had said, "You never *used* to get so upset about losing things," as he was leaving.

"I never used to *lose* things," she'd replied tartly. And refrained from adding, "And I didn't *lose* what I'm looking for. Someone *took* it."

LuAnn answered, "No, I didn't tell anyone about Brownie's wallet," and sat down on her bed. "Why?"

"Someone took it. It's gone."

LuAnn just laughed. "Oh, Katie, who would take a dirty old wallet? It's probably just buried under all your clutter. I mean, just look at this room. It's a pigsty!"

Katie was offended. Why couldn't people take her seriously? Okay, so she hadn't been *acting* like the kind of person people took seriously, since . . . since that day on the river. She'd give them that. But didn't she seem serious *now*? Couldn't they tell the difference? "You could always move out," she told LuAnn, her voice stiff with hurt.

"I've been thinking about it." LuAnn looked up at Katie and said, "You've changed a lot. I guess it's understandable, after what happened, but . . ."

"Never mind," Katie interrupted. "It's okay. I don't blame you. Just tell me this, though." She picked up the silver frame and held it in front of LuAnn. "Did you do this?"

LuAnn looked at the picture. "Wow, great shot of Brownie. Did I do what?"

Katie tapped impatiently on the frame. "Did you put this picture in here?"

LuAnn sat up straighter. "What are you talking about?"

"I didn't put this picture in here. It isn't even *my* picture. So what I want to know is, did *you* do it?"

The expression on LuAnn's face was blank. "No. Didn't *you*? It's *your* frame, isn't it?"

Katie sighed. "LuAnn, if I'd put this picture into this frame, I would hardly be asking you if *you'd* done it, would I?"

But she could see in LuAnn's wide blue eyes that LuAnn wasn't at all sure just what Katie Sullivan might do next.

"I don't tamper with other people's things,"

LuAnn said coldly, standing up. "You shouldn't even be asking me if I did something like that." She whirled and stalked into the bathroom, slamming the door so hard, the posters on the walls fluttered and Katie's Salem U pennant slipped sideways.

LuAnn stayed in the bathroom a long time.

Still chilled to the bone from her terror in the pool, and feeling lonely and misunderstood, Katie climbed into bed without undressing, huddling in a ball under the covers.

Someone had been in their room. Someone had touched her things and taken Brownie's wallet.

LuAnn came out of the bathroom and padded over to her bed.

"I'm sorry," Katie said quietly.

"Forget it." But LuAnn's voice was brusque.

Katie sighed. LuAnn would be shopping for a new roommate tomorrow.

Who could blame her?

And did it really matter how the picture of Brownie had slipped into the silver frame or what had happened to the muddy wallet? Someone had tried to *drown* her tonight. That was far more terrifying than the thought of someone messing around in her room.

Her attacker had failed, though. She had managed to get away.

This time . . .

Would he try again?

The next morning, LuAnn awoke cheerful, acting as if nothing out of the ordinary had happened between them. When she left for class, she called out breezily, "See you at Nightmare Hall later. Linda's party is at seven. I'm going straight there after classes. 'Bye."

Linda's party? Katie had forgotten. The last thing she felt like doing was celebrating someone's birthday. Silly hats, candles on a cake, people expecting her to smile and talk. Not now, not today. Celebrating *anything* was out of the question.

But . . . if she could slip away from the party for a few minutes, she could run up to the attic at Nightmare Hall and hunt for that missing garment bag, the one with the hatpin slit down the front. It had to be up there somewhere. Hidden away, of course, so that no one would believe her crazy story. Except . . . it *wasn't* crazy. If she could find the bag, she could convince everyone that she'd been telling the truth.

Then maybe, just maybe, they'd believe that she also had almost been drowned in the pool and that someone wanted her dead.

Finding that bag was her only hope of being believed.

She would go to the party.

Katie rode to Nightmare Hall with Callie, Allen, and Davis. It was quiet in the car. The air seemed strained between Callie and Davis in the front seat, and in the backseat, Allen kept asking Katie if she was okay.

"Will you *stop* asking me that?" she finally hissed. "You're making me feel like an invalid. I'm *fine!*"

But she wasn't. The thought of actually walking into Nightmare Hall, where she'd come so close to drawing her last breath, made her physically ill. If Allen didn't believe that the attack had actually happened, why was he so concerned about her?

As if she didn't know. What he was concerned about was her sanity, not her safety.

Wounded by her irritation, Allen said quietly, "I'm just worried about you, that's all."

"Well, quit it!" Katie turned her head to glare at him. "And if you open your mouth and say that I didn't *used* to mind you worrying about me, I'll jump out of this car."

Allen subsided into a sullen silence.

Fortunately, the ride was a short one.

A well-known member of the swim team, Linda Carlyle was popular for her cheerful, friendly personality as well. Nightmare Hall was teeming with Salem students. They seemed, Katie thought as she nervously entered the big front hall, to be having a blast. The big old house shook with music and laughter.

The size of the crowd would make it easier for her to slip upstairs to the attic unnoticed. Well, Allen would probably notice. But after the way she'd bitten off his head in the car, he should know better than to come looking for her.

So, when Linda attracted everyone's attention by announcing a wild, "treasure" hunt on the grounds around the house, Katie seized the opportunity to slip upstairs.

She was almost unable to walk into the attic. Her bones and muscles turned to mud when she was facing the narrow little door. She had almost *died* in there. Wasn't she crazy to go back in?

No. She *had* to try to find that missing garment bag.

But she pulled the door open very slowy, and peered inside, listening for the tiniest sound that would tell her the attic wasn't empty.

She heard nothing. Everyone was downstairs.

Slowly, carefully, her breath coming in irregular spurts, she moved on into the attic.

She propped the closet door open so that she could see by the light she turned on in there, hoping no one outside would notice the faint yellow glow coming from the fourth floor.

Then she began her own "scavenger hunt."

Although she hurriedly dug into boxes and trunks and pawed through shelves, she found no sign of a large white clothing bag, shaped like a refrigerator, a long, narrow slit trailing down its front next to the zipper.

She *knew* the damaged bag had been hidden somewhere. But it hadn't been hidden in the attic, that was clear.

Discouraged, Katie turned off the closet light and went downstairs.

The house was empty. Silence had replaced the music, talk, and laughter. Everyone was outside scavenging. Brief flashes of yellow light passed the long, narrow dining room windows as people carrying small flashlights ran by in search of treasure.

Wishing she'd gone outside with them instead of wasting all that time in the attic, Katie sank into a dining room chair. A three-tier, white-frosted birthday cake sat in the center of the table. The top was decorated with a fig-

ure in a blue swimsuit, poised to dive in
pling waves of blue icing. Red balloons hu
from the chandelier, red crepe paper streamers
were thumbtacked into each of four corners of
the ceiling and draped across the room to meet
at the chandelier. Goofy, silly pictures of Linda
adorned the walls.

Very festive, Katie thought. LuAnn did a
good job. I should have helped. I used to do
stuff like that all the time. Maybe it would have
taken my mind off everything else.

Nervous about being alone in the big, old
house, she was about to jump up and join the
hunt outside when music suddenly began to fill
the big dining room. A second or two later,
someone began singing, loudly and joyfully,
*"Happy birthday to you, happy birthday to
you . . ."*

Katie's first thought was that it was bad timing on someone's part. The birthday girl wasn't
even in the house.

And then, in almost the same instant, she
recognized the voice.

Her mouth fell open and her backbone deserted her and slowly, without a sound, she
slid to the floor.

As Brownie's voice, clear and confident, sang
on, *"Happy birthday to you-oo, happy birthday
to you!"*

Chapter 14

Katie was still slumped on the dining room carpet when LuAnn came bursting in through the front door, followed by the crowd of party guests. Seeing her roommate half-sitting, half-lying against a chair, her eyes closed, LuAnn cried out and rushed to Katie's side.

While Davis took Katie's pulse, Callie ran into the kitchen for a wet cloth. Everyone else gathered around Davis and Katie.

She opened her eyes to find all of the party guests standing in a large semicircle, staring down at her. Cringing in embarrassment, she sat up, straightening the folds of her blue skirt around her legs. "Could you please get these people out of here?" she murmured to Davis, who was still holding her wrist. "I feel like a zoo exhibit!"

"What happened? Did you fall?"

"No. I . . . I think maybe I fainted. Would you *please* make them leave?"

"Okay, everybody!" he called, standing up, "show's over. She's okay now."

Sensing Katie's embarrassment, Jessica Vogt urged the guests into the library, where, she said, a roaring fire blazed in the fireplace. "C'mon you guys. It's almost time to cut the cake and sing 'Happy Birthday.'"

Her remark reminded Katie of what she had heard that had made her slide to the floor. She groaned. Brownie . . . singing . . . no, it couldn't be. But . . . she had *heard* it.

When the others had gone and only Allen, Davis, Callie, and LuAnn were surrounding her, Katie pulled herself up to sit on a chair. "I heard Brownie singing," she said quietly, her head down. She couldn't bear to see the expressions on their faces when she shared this latest bit of news with them, but she *had* to tell someone. She was sick to death of keeping things to herself. "He was singing 'Happy Birthday.'"

"*What* did she say?" LuAnn asked Davis. "I thought she said . . ."

He nodded. "She did. She said she heard . . . Brownie singing." To Katie, he said, "Did anyone else hear it?"

Her head flew up. "No! Does that make you happy? That no one heard it but me?"

Allen warned, "Katie, take it easy," and Callie said worriedly, "She thinks she heard Brownie singing? 'Happy Birthday?' But — "

"I know!" Katie cried, jumping to her feet. "I know I couldn't have! But I *did*!"

"Who was he singing it to?" Allen asked calmly.

Katie looked at him. "What?"

"Well, when he got to the middle part where you sing, 'Happy Birthday, dear so-and-so,' whose name did he sing? He hardly knew Linda, so . . ."

"Oh." Katie thought for a minute, trying to remember. "I . . . I don't think he said a name. I think he just sang, 'Happy birthday, happy birthday', instead of saying a name. But . . . I'm not sure. I was . . . upset."

"I'll bet," Davis said sympathetically. "Look, are you sure it was Brownie's voice? I mean, you just said you were upset. So how can you be sure whose voice it was?"

"Davis, I *don't* get upset when I hear 'Happy Birthday'. I was *upset* because it was *Brownie's* voice singing it. Wouldn't you have been?"

"It had to be a joke," Allen suggested, coming up behind Katie to lay a comforting hand on her shoulders. "A gag."

Katie stiffened. "I hope I don't have the kind of friends who would think something so disgusting is *funny*. I certainly didn't find it funny."

But she could see that no one in the room could imagine what it had felt like, hearing that voice so loud and clear, singing away happily. Pain had rolled over her in waves and she hadn't been able to catch her breath. She had known, even then, that it couldn't be real, but there it was, in her ears, and there was no question that the singer was Brownie. No question at all.

"This isn't the first time I've heard him," she said, wondering even as she spoke if she was making a terrible mistake. "I heard him in my room one night."

"Singing?" Davis asked. There was concern in his dark eyes . . . concern for *her*.

She was humiliated. "No, not singing . . . oh, never mind, forget it!" This wasn't working. She couldn't really blame them . . . how *could* they believe her? She had trouble believing it herself. *Could* she have imagined it? She'd been upset about not finding the bag in the attic, and nervous about being alone in Nightmare Hall . . . "I was probably dreaming . . . *both* times. I probably fell asleep here at the table because I haven't been sleeping lately, and while I was sleeping, I had a dream. Look, since I can't think of any more ways to make a fool of myself just now, I think I'll leave before something comes to mind. I'm going back to the dorm and sack out. LuAnn, tell Linda I'm sorry, okay?" Katie shrugged. "On second thought, she probably won't even know I'm gone. I'll see you guys tomorrow. Have fun!"

"I'm coming with you," Allen said, leaving no room for argument.

She *was* a little shaky. Having someone walk with her might be a good idea. As long as Allen didn't remind her that she never *used* to faint.

Davis offered to drive both of them back to campus. "No, you stay here," Katie said, remembering the concern in his eyes. She couldn't stand the thought of anyone feeling sorry for her, least of all Davis. And realized for the first time that she would have preferred that Davis feel something entirely different for her.

That surprised her. Davis? Okay, so he and Callie weren't an item anymore. But he was just a friend. Wasn't he?

Had that been real concern in his eyes? For her? Or . . . or was it just pity? Because she seemed to be one glove short of a pair?

Then shame welled up inside Katie. What

was she thinking? Romance? What about Brownie? It hadn't been that long. Maybe there was something really wrong with her.

She didn't want to talk about anything that had happened, but on the way back to campus, Allen asked her one question after another.

She answered honestly, telling him how she'd felt about the word GUILTY being scrawled in the dust on her car, and the gas tank being emptied. She told him about hearing Brownie's voice in her room. She even told him what the voice had said. That it was her fault.

"*What* was your fault?" Allen asked.

Katie shrugged as they trudged up the highway toward campus. "That he died, I guess. Trying to save me. I mean, wouldn't you think that's what he meant?"

"No." Allen shook his head. "He couldn't have meant that. Because he's dead. Dead people don't tell you something is your fault." He uttered a short, humorless laugh. "Dead people don't tell you anything. You know that."

She should have talked to someone about all of this sooner. Davis had been right. It did help.

"You were dreaming," Allen went on. "Pure and simple. Don't do it again, okay?"

Katie laughed. That was Allen . . . everything was so easy, so uncomplicated for him. She'd had a bad dream, it had upset her . . .

so she just shouldn't have that dream again.

If only it *were* that simple. But she'd had another one of those "dreams" tonight at Linda's party, when she hadn't even known she was asleep. So it probably wasn't something she had any control over.

What a horrible, terrifying thought! If she couldn't stop herself from hearing Brownie's voice, she really *would* go mad.

"This is too depressing," she said. "I don't want to talk about this stuff anymore. Let's go up on the tower!" The tower was the tallest building on campus, and Katie loved the view.

"The tower? Not on your life! You'll do something nutty like dancing on the eighteenth-story terrace wall."

"Not a bad idea," Katie said lightly, grinning. "And why not?" Dancing on an eighteenth-story wall was just the sort of thing that Brownie would have applauded. Then she remembered that doing *that* sort of thing was exactly what kept people from believing her now. It was her own fault that she felt so alone.

"Because it's stupid, that's why not. You're just lucky you didn't get pneumonia when you went crazy in the fountain."

Although she knew he was right, his tone of voice annoyed her. "You sound like someone's mother! Did you ever know a single kid who got pneumonia because he got his feet wet on a cold day?"

Allen laughed. "No. And I'm not your mother, or your father, either. And," he added, "I'm not your brother, which is what a lot of people in high school thought I was."

"They did? I never knew that." She glanced sideways at him. "So, did you hate that? Having people think I was related to you?"

"Why would I hate it? Listen, I have an idea." Allen stopped on the berm of the highway. Across the road, cars peeled in and out of the parking lot for Burgers Etc. "Let's go over to the diner, get a burger, and I'll tell you all about it."

Why not? She wasn't keen on going back to her room alone. And, for the first time in a long time, she suddenly felt hungry. Maybe it was from not feeling so alone. "Deal."

When they were seated in the warm, crowded diner, and had given their order to the waitress, Allen said casually, "Maybe you should think about transferring. Get away from some of the bad memories."

"Transfer?"

"Sure." Allen nodded, and a clump of pale blond hair fell across his forehed. He pushed it back impatiently. "You could go to State. I'd even transfer with you, if it would make you feel better. My folks would be thrilled. They wanted me to go there in the first place. It's cheaper, and it's closer to home. And your parents wouldn't mind. They'd like having you only thirty minutes away, right?"

Katie toyed with her silverware. If she were going to transfer, she would have done it when Brownie died. She'd been home for two weeks then. She'd thought about it long and hard, and had finally decided that going back was the right thing to do, the thing she *wanted* to do.

"Allen, I don't want to leave Salem."

He leaned back against the blue leatherette seat. "Well, I just thought . . . with everything that's happened here, you'd rather be somewhere else. But if you don't want to, it's okay." He smiled at her, his blue eyes warm. "I'm not really keen on leaving, either. Now."

She knew he was referring to Callie. Allen and Callie would be great together. If it troubled Katie, just a little, that a relationship with Callie might make Allen less accessible to *her*, she quickly pushed the thought away as selfish and shallow.

Someone played a song on the jukebox, and when the music began, Katie had one tiny, frightening moment when she expected to hear Brownie's voice bursting into song at any second. Her breath caught in her chest until a female voice began singing.

She felt stupid and silly. And relieved.

Then Davis, LuAnn, and Callie arrived, the party over, and pushed into the booth occupied by Katie and Allen.

They talked about everything except what Katie had heard in the dining room at Nightmare Hall.

Or *thought* she'd heard.

Chapter 15

Over the next few days, Katie saw Allen and Callie together often, on campus, at Vinnie's, walking together in the mall, holding hands. Although she was happy for them, the sight of them so lost in each other filled her with a sad longing. She missed both of them. And she missed something else . . . that happiness of knowing she had someone in her life who cared a lot just for her.

Yet, she found herself avoiding Davis. It seemed so disloyal to Brownie to be interested in someone else so soon.

"What's so fascinating about that guy at the counter?" he said, frowning down at her.

"What guy? What are you talking about?"

"That guy you've had your eyes on ever since he walked in. The one in the blue shirt."

"Brownie, I wasn't watching any guy. I was just . . . daydreaming." She did that a lot,

always had. It bothered people, made them think she wasn't listening to them. They said, "That Kit, she's so quiet, you never know what she's thinking." Brownie, especially, hated it. He liked to know exactly what people were thinking, so he could deal with it head on. She tried, all the time, to change, but she wasn't having much luck. Quiet was who she was. More and more often lately, she wanted to say, "If you don't like who I am, find somebody else." But, of course, she never did. Because then she'd lose him.

"I don't even know who that guy is, Brownie."

His cheeks flushed. "Don't kid a kidder. And don't ever mistake me for a fool, Kit. That's one thing I'm not."

She turned away from the guy in the blue shirt. But she wondered if anyone else ever saw that anger in Brownie, or if she was the only one.

Later, he'd apologized, saying it was only because he loved her.

She had liked hearing that, but she couldn't help wondering what it was about her that he loved, since there seemed to be so many things about her that annoyed him these days. No one else noticed . . . only her. Everyone else thought they made a wonderful couple. And so, most *of the time it was easy for her to tell herself that they were still blissfully happy.*

But in her darker moments, she knew that the only way she could keep Brownie was to change, to become more outgoing, more fun, more exciting . . . like him.

And so she kept trying, even though Davis said, "You are who you are. You'll go nuts trying to be somebody else."

It seemed ironic to Katie now, sitting alone in her room late one evening, that she finally *had* changed. But not only was it too late, it didn't seem to be doing her much good. Just the opposite. She was getting into trouble on and off campus, her grades were disastrous, and now her roommate had moved out. LuAnn had moved in with Linda, at Nightmare Hall. LuAnn had decided a gloomy old off-campus dorm was preferable to living with someone who was so unpredictable, and saw and heard things that weren't there.

Katie understood why LuAnn had moved out, and she didn't blame her. But her timing stank. When had there been a worse time for Katie to be alone?

She had successfully hidden her fear when she got back to the room on Monday, and found LuAnn all packed and ready to go. But inside, Katie was quaking. Alone . . . all alone . . .

now . . . when she *knew* someone wanted her dead. And probably knew where she lived.

"I'm sorry, Katie," LuAnn said as she turned to leave, suitcases in hand. Linda had come to help with the moving, and stood in the doorway, looking uncomfortable. "It might be nice to have a single for a change. Or you can always get another roommate. Our RA will help."

True. But Katie didn't want a single right now. She had already spoken to the Resident Advisor on their floor. She had offered to help. But the way she had said it told Katie a lot. People weren't going to be lined up around the Quad to move in with someone who was, as Allen put it recently, "a loose cannon." Oh, sure, they liked *watching* her dance in the fountain. They even cheered her on. But that wasn't at all the same as *living* with her.

As LuAnn turned and left, it took every ounce of self-discipline Katie possessed to keep from shouting, "No! Please don't go! Don't leave me here alone, not now!" What stopped her was the thought of the looks on her and Linda's faces if she did that.

Life was too short to beg. Let them go. She'd manage. She'd manage just fine, dammit!

Or die trying . . .

That was exactly what she was afraid of.

But Allen and Callie and Davis were still

there for her. They wouldn't let anything horrible happen to her, if they could help it.

If. . . .

She would just have to spend as little time in her room as possible. When she wasn't at the river, there were parties and movies and dances and meets and games to go to. There was safety in numbers, wasn't there? If Allen and Callie and Davis weren't available, she'd find other people to go with. This was a college campus, for pete's sake, there were always people who wanted to party. All she had to do was find them. It was important that she be surrounded by people at all times. That way, she'd be safe. Unless . . .

Unless one of those people turned out to be her executioner.

If only she knew who it *was*. . . . *who* hated her so much. No one had ever hated her before. It was a terrible, horrible feeling, knowing that someone was that angry with her. Someone out there wanted her *dead*.

If only other people believed he was out there, too. That would help. *She* knew he was out there . . . somewhere. But what good did that do, if no one else knew it?

She should be doing something about it, taking charge of her life, stopping anything worse from happening. But every time she racked her brain, trying to come up with answers, she ran into a blank wall. If she had found the damaged garment bag, that would have helped. But . . . she had no idea what to do next.

On her first night alone, Katie called Callie and talked her into going to Vinnie's to eat. At Vinnie's, they could hang out most of the evening if they wanted to. They could stretch dinner into an entire evening, and she wouldn't have to go back to her room until late.

She expected Callie to bring Allen, but she was surprised when Davis showed up at Katie's dorm room, too. No one mentioned LuAnn's departure when they glanced at the empty bed. Katie was grateful for their tact. She didn't think she could talk about it without getting upset. And that would wreck the vow she'd taken that afternoon to *not* get upset about *anything* in front of other people, no matter *what* she heard or saw . . . or *thought* she heard or saw. No way. She was going to be the picture of composure from now on. . . . at least, in front of other people. If she was suddenly overtaken by the urge to fall apart, she'd do it in the privacy of her own room. It was the only way to get them to take her seriously.

At Vinnie's, when they had placed their order, and Allen and Callie had gone off to play a game of pool, Davis asked her how she was feeling.

Swamped by that horrid "invalid" feeling again, Katie answered archly, "Fine. I'm just fine." Then she added boldly, "I'd feel a whole lot better, though, if I didn't feel like everyone in here was staring at me. I can almost hear them saying, 'There's that girl who says she got trapped in Nightmare Hall's attic.' The key word there being, 'says.' Like it really *didn't* happen, except in my head."

Davis shook his head. "How do you know they're not staring at you because you look gorgeous in that red shirt?"

Katie bristled. "Davis, please don't try to talk like Brownie. You're not very good at it."

His cheeks deepened in color, but his voice was calm. "Why not? Haven't you been trying to *act* like him? And it's driving you nuts, just like I told you it would. Why don't you just go back to being who you really are, Katie? You were . . . okay . . . just the way you were."

Shaking, she stood up. "The way I *was*," she whispered angrily, "is what *killed* him!"

She would have turned and left then, but Davis, too, jumped to his feet. Grabbing her hand to keep her from running, he said grimly, "No! No, that's *not* why he died. He died because he was foolish and irresponsible. He never should have gone out on the river that day. And face it, Katie, he never should have risked your life as well as his own."

"He didn't mean to," she said softly.

"No, I know he didn't. That was part of Brownie's charm." He reached out with one hand and tipped her chin upward. "You have to stop beating yourself up about what happened. We've all watched it happening, and we don't know how to stop it. You're not guilty of anything except loving Brownie."

She looked straight at him with solemn eyes. "Someone," she said clearly, "doesn't agree with you. But since none of you believe that, I don't want to talk about this anymore. I have to go to the ladies' room." And she retrieved her hand and left him standing there beside the booth.

When she came back, Allen and Callie had rejoined Davis. Katie acted as if nothing had taken place, smiling and talking to Davis as she always had.

I'm getting good at this, she thought with pleasure, I'm getting very good at pretending nothing is wrong when everything is. Academy Awards, here I come!

But she felt like weeping.

By the time they returned to the Quad, the dorm had quieted down. Allen and Davis left, saying they had studying to do, but Katie talked Callie into studying with her. She had a philosophy assignment overdue, and she and Callie were in the same class. "You can give me some pointers," she said, as Callie dropped her backpack and books on LuAnn's empty bed.

"Yeah, right. I hate that class. Underhill is boring. I have to fight to stay awake in there. Someone should tell him that the study of philosophy isn't supposed to include his own personal theories about the universe, especially when they're about as exciting as stale bread."

Katie laughed. It was going to be nice, having someone in the room with her. Maybe she could even talk Callie into spending the night. That might be fun.

If she didn't wake Callie up in the middle of the night, screaming from one of her nightmares . . .

Saying she couldn't study without coffee, Callie went downstairs to get it. Katie rescued her own backpack from the floor and dug into its depths for her philosophy book and notebook.

The book wasn't inside the backpack.

Katie groaned. She'd left it somewhere. The library? Callie would think she was a real airhead. And she'd probably tell Allen that Katie would lose her head if it wasn't securely fastened to her neck.

Well, things could be worse. At least they were both in the same class. She could share Callie's book.

Katie opened Callie's red backpack. As she unbuckled and lifted the flap, two small, thin audio cassettes in clear plastic cases fell out and slid to the floor.

Katie bent to pick them up. She would have slipped them back into the backpack and continued looking for the textbook, except for one thing.

The cassettes were labeled.

Each had a white label taped to the front.

And each said the same thing:

BROWNIE.

Tapes of Brownie?

Katie held them in her hands, studying them. Tapes of Brownie? *What* tapes of Brownie? Callie had never said that she had tapes of Brownie. Wouldn't she have mentioned it somewhere along the way?

Maybe . . . Katie turned the tapes over and over in her hand, as if by doing so, she would learn what was on them . . . maybe Brownie had sent audio tapes to Callie when she was a freshman, instead of writing her letters. Most boys hated writing letters, didn't they? But he would have missed his older sister, the first year she'd been away from home. They were so close. So maybe he'd sat down, on those rare evenings when he wasn't out partying, and talked into a cassette recorder, just as if Callie were sitting across from him. And mailed the tapes to her, just as if they were letters.

If Brownie's voice was on those tapes, Katie wanted to hear it. Callie wouldn't mind. If the conversations weren't too private, maybe Callie would let her borrow them to make copies. So that she, too, could listen to him once in a while when she was especially missing him.

Tapes in hand, Katie turned to her portable cassette player and thrust the first tape into place.

Her breathing was shallow with anticipation as she pushed the ON button.

She had to wait only a second or two. Then, there it was, Brownie's deep, confident voice filling the room. But . . . Katie sat up straighter, her eyes widening . . . Brownie wasn't talking to his sister on the tape.

He was singing.

And what he was singing was, "Happy birthday to you, happy birthday to you . . ."

Exactly as she'd heard it in Nightingale Hall's dining room.

She didn't *want* to hear that.

What was it doing on this tape?

Katie jumped off the bed and slammed the OFF button. She yanked the tape from the player, and hesitated only for a moment before inserting the second tape and pushing the ON button again.

And then she gasped and her hands flew to her mouth as Brownie's voice began again, talking this time instead of singing.

But he wasn't saying, "Hi, sis, how are you? You know how I hate writing letters, but I was kind of missing you . . . hard to believe, I know, but there you are . . . so I thought I'd just spout a few words on tape for posterity. When I'm rich and famous, you can sell these tapes for a small fortune."

He wasn't saying anything like that.

What he was saying was, "It's all your fault . . . it's all your fault . . . it's all your fault," with only a slight pause in between each phrase. Over and over again, just as she'd heard it that night. . . .

Accusing . . . accusing *her*.

Guilty . . . guilty . . .

Suddenly, a different voice broke in. "What on earth do you think you're doing?"

Katie's head came up. Callie, her eyes filled with horror, stood in the doorway.

"Callie?" Katie questioned, rising to her feet. "Callie? It was *you*?"

Chapter 16

Callie, her face bone-white, moved on into the room, closing the door behind her. She sat down on LuAnn's bed. "What were you doing looking in my backpack?"

"Trying to find a book." Katie reached out and extracted the second tape from the cassette player. "Instead, I . . . I found these." She moved backward to sit down on her own bed. "It was you! I can't believe it! You . . . you played these tapes so that I would think . . . what? That Brownie was haunting me? Or that I was losing my mind? Or both? Why, Callie? I don't understand . . ."

Callie jumped up and began pacing the small room, her cheeks red, wringing her hands in agitation. "You got off scot-free! It's your *fault* my brother's dead . . . he's gone . . . *gone* . . . I'll never see him again, and it's your fault. But nothing ever *happened* to you! You weren't punished. You just walked away. Somebody had to *do* something. So I did it, and I'm not sorry. Not sorry at all."

Bewilderment overcame Katie. "But you said . . . you said you didn't blame me. You said it was an accident."

"I lied. If you'd known how angry I was, you'd have guessed right away that it was me. So I had to pretend." Callie's face twisted angrily. "I *hated* that! Pretending that I didn't blame you . . . it was so *hard!*"

"But . . ." Katie didn't dare take her eyes off Callie. She was so *angry*. Any second now, that awful anger could take over and send her flying at Katie. Callie was a big, strong girl. Strong enough to almost drown someone in a pool.

Stall, Katie told herself, stall for time . . . "Where . . . where did you get those tapes? Of Brownie?"

"He sent me the 'Happy Birthday' tape last year. I just edited it to remove my name."

"And the other one? The one where . . ." Katie's voice quavered ". . . where he says it's my fault?"

"That's from last summer. From our answering machine at home." Callie continued to pace, back and forth, back and forth, spitting out her words. "Brownie took the car one day after I'd had it all afternoon. I was supposed to get gas, but I forgot. He ran out of gas on the freeway, and called home to yell at me. Said he was going to be late for a party, and it was all my fault. I took the tape so my parents wouldn't know I'd forgotten to fill the tank, and then when Brownie came home, I bribed him not to tell them. I still had that tape. All I had to do was edit it to make him keep repeating that one phrase: it's all your fault, it's all your fault. I couldn't believe how perfect it was. Exactly what I needed."

Katie glanced around the room. "But . . . I heard it *here* . . . in this room! How . . . ?"

Callie stopped her pacing. "I was here." She pointed. "Over there, next to the door. LuAnn had told me she was going to stay at Nightmare Hall with Linda. I hid in the stairwell, watching through the door window until LuAnn left. There weren't any lights on in here, so I just slipped in and knelt inside the door in the dark. You were in bed, and you couldn't see me. Too dark. And it's not like I was sitting right in front of you. I wasn't there that long. I couldn't tell what time it was, and I was afraid it would get light before I got out of there. So I left. I'd done what I came to do. And I knew it had worked."

The room fell silent briefly. Callie, looking

drained, went back over and sat down on LuAnn's bed again.

"And you . . . drained my gas tank? You wrote GUILTY on my car? You took my wallet and switched it to my backpack? God, Callie, I don't *believe* this! You were torturing me! I thought I was losing my mind, and so did everyone else. And you just let them think it! You . . . you switched the picture of my parents with the one of Brownie?"

"I didn't write GUILTY on your car. Someone else must have done that. I was in the theater with you, remember? But, yeah, I did the other things. You had it coming. I watched you partying and having a high old time. You didn't seem to care at all that Brownie was gone. Not at *all*!"

Katie tried to judge the distance between her bed and the door. It wasn't that far. But Callie was sitting right in the middle of that path to the door. She would never let Katie get by her.

"I just wanted you to suffer," Callie said sullenly. "That's all. It wasn't right that you weren't suffering, not right at all."

But Katie wasn't listening. Enlightenment filled her eyes. "You . . . you did all of those things to me so that. . . . so that everyone would think I was losing my mind. That way, no one would ever believe me when I told them about the attic and about the pool. *That's* why you did it! And it *worked*!"

Callie frowned. "What are you talking about? I was trying to punish you, not scare you. I already told you that. How was I supposed to know you were going to go off the deep end and make up crazy stories about the attic at Nightmare Hall?"

"Crazy stories?" Katie flushed angrily. "That's very funny, coming from *you*! You know better than anyone that I was telling the truth about what happened. Since you were *there*!" She glanced sideways at her bedside table. Was there anything in that pile of clutter that would help her? Anything she could use to keep Callie from finishing the job she'd begun in the attic, and then again in the pool? A nail file . . . maybe . . .

"I was there?" Callie stared at her. "I was *where*?"

"In the attic. Tell me, Callie, did I really hit my head on a beam? Or did *you* put out my lights, as well as the light in the closet? What did you hit me with? It felt like a huge log. And where did my elbow connect in the pool? I thought I hit a jaw, but I don't see any bruises. Or are you hiding them under makeup?"

Why did the telephone have to be on Lu-

Ann's table, instead of her own? If she made a move toward it, Callie would grab it . . . or *her*.

"You think that I . . ." Callie looked stunned. "You think that I tried to *kill* you? How could you think that? How could you possibly think that?"

Of course she'd deny it, Katie thought. "But you just said . . ."

"Katie, get a grip!" Callie said scornfully. "You really *are* losing it. First of all, I don't even know what you mean by the *pool*. Did someone attack you there? I'm a crummy swimmer, so it certainly wasn't *me*. Brownie was the swimmer in our family. As for the attic, I didn't even know you were up there. No one did."

"*Someone* did!" Katie shouted.

"Okay, okay. But it wasn't me. I can't believe you'd think I would . . . *kill* someone. Or try to. Or even *want* to. God, Katie, what do you think I am? Yes, I did the other stuff . . . I wanted you to be as miserable as I was. But . . . but I never *attacked* you! I swear I didn't."

She sounded like . . . like she was telling the truth. And why would she admit to everything else but lie about the pool and the attic? Wouldn't she want to brag about how she had terrified Katie? Of course she would. So . . . she had to be telling the truth.

But . . . if it hadn't been Callie . . . then who?

"Are you going to tell?" Callie asked. She seemed drained. Her face was very pale. "About the things I did to you? You could get me kicked out of school. I wouldn't blame you." Callie sighed. "Davis warned me . . ."

Katie jerked upright. "Davis knew what you were doing?"

"Oh, no, of course not. But he knew I blamed you. He kept telling me I was being unfair, that it wasn't your fault. We argued about it all the time. And finally, he'd had it with the way I went on and on about you. He said he didn't want to see me again until I got over it. Only I *didn't* get over it, so. . . . And then, Allen came along and he was so nice, it didn't matter so much about Davis anymore."

Katie nodded, still trying to take it all in. "Allen can be a good friend."

"So can Davis. Did you know that he keeps a picture of you and Brownie in his wallet? I saw it at Vinnie's one night when Davis was paying the bill."

"A picture? Of me and Brownie? What picture?"

"You know, that one I took of the two of you the day of the tennis match."

But . . . but there were only *two* of those. One was in Katie's wallet. The other had been in Brownie's wallet, until the river snatched it free.

Could Davis have found Brownie's wallet, removed the picture, and then buried the wallet again?

No, that was crazy.

"Callie," Katie said hesitantly, "that picture . . . the one in Davis's wallet . . . is it . . . is it by any chance all wrinkled and messy?"

"Messy? No, why would it be messy?"

"Because, I should have told you before . . . I *found* Brownie's wallet. In the riverbank. And the only picture missing was that one. There were only two wallet-sized photos of that picture, Callie. I have one. The other one was in Brownie's wallet. And now it isn't. If the river ripped it free, how could Davis possibly have it?"

Callie didn't know. "Where is the wallet? Could I have it?"

"It's gone. Someone took it. It's gone." After a minute or two, Katie said, "Callie, you're wrong. About me not caring. I was dying inside, just like you. But if I'd stopped to think about what happened, I would have agreed with you . . . thinking that it was *my* fault. I just couldn't — So I tried to stay too busy to think. It was the only way I could handle things. Can you understand that?"

"Kit . . . Katie," Callie said, tears forming in her eyes, "you can report me if you want to. I wouldn't blame you. But suddenly, now that it's all out in the open, I don't feel so angry anymore. I'm too tired."

"Me too," Katie said, nodding.

"So . . . I know I've got a lot of nerve asking, but do you think maybe you could . . . forgive me? We were friends once. I know Brownie would be furious if he knew what I'd done, but I don't think he'd want us to be enemies forever, do you?"

"No. I know he wouldn't." Callie had hurt her, a lot, and scared her, and made her think she was losing her mind. But she'd done it out of her own hurt. And she *hadn't* tried to kill her. . . .

Katie's heart sank. Although she was safe here and now, in this room, with this person sitting opposite her . . . she wasn't safe anywhere *else*.

Her attacker was still out there . . . her executioner . . .

"I'll make a deal with you," Katie said, more bravely than she felt. "I'll forgive you, and I won't report you, either . . . we'll keep it between us . . . *if* you'll spend the night tonight." She forced a small laugh. "You just might find out that that's punishment enough. LuAnn certainly thought it was too much."

"Are you sure? You trust me enough to have me sleep over?"

Katie thought about that for a minute. Callie had done awful things. But . . . they had both loved the same person. And that person would hate it if he knew they no longer trusted each other.

"Yes," she said firmly. "I do. And I'd appreciate it if you'd stay. I really would."

"Thanks, Katie," Callie said softly. "Let me just call Allen and tell him. He was going to call me later at my dorm. He'll get worried if I'm not there."

Katie laughed. "Yeah, you're right. He will. And when you're done on the phone, I'm going to call Davis and ask him where he got that picture. The one of Brownie and me."

But when she dialed and asked for Davis at his dorm, she was told he wasn't there.

It was awfully late. She wondered where he was.

She would have to wait until tomorrow.

She was about to climb into bed when Callie suddenly appeared beside her. "Katie," she said, "I'm really sorry. For everything. And I believe that something terrible happened to you in the attic, and in the pool. I'll do anything I can to help you find out who hurt you. Allen and Davis will, too, I'm sure."

"Thanks, Callie. That means a lot." Katie smiled.

And although Katie still had no idea who or why someone was trying to kill her, and knew that she would have to face that all over again the next day, she focused on the fact that she wasn't going to be alone all night long, and was able to sleep.

Chapter 17

When Katie awoke the following morning, Callie was already dressed and ready to leave. She was sitting on LuAnn's bed, books in hand.

"I've got an eight o'clock," she said when Katie had struggled awake. "But I wanted to make sure you were okay before I left. About . . . about us, I mean."

Katie nodded. "It's okay, Callie. Thanks for staying last night. I didn't wake you up with a nightmare, did I?"

"No." Callie turned to leave, and then turned back again. "I know you don't like to talk about Brownie, but . . ."

Why did they all think *she* didn't want to talk about it? They were the ones who changed the subject every time she mentioned his name. "Go ahead."

"Well, you talked last night about that picture being missing from Brownie's wallet. I'm not surprised. The police said he was really knocked around by the river that day. Had a terrible gash on his skull when they found him."

Katie struggled upright in bed, her eyes on Callie's face. "A gash? What from?"

Callie shrugged. "Probably a rock in the river. You know how vicious the current was that day, Katie. If it hadn't been, Brownie would have made it to shore."

A picture of Brownie slamming into a rock, cracking his head open, assailed Katie. She felt sick. "That gash on his head . . . is that what killed him?" she asked weakly. "He . . . he didn't drown?"

"No, he *did* drown." Callie was very pale. "I guess what happened is, he was slammed up against that rock, knocked unconscious, and then drowned. That's what one police officer said."

Images swam in Katie's head, worse than any she'd had in her nightmares.

"I didn't mean to upset you," Callie said.

"No, it's okay." At last she had an explanation for why Brownie hadn't made it to shore. He'd hit his head.

Katie waited for a sense of relief, a feeling of freedom that should have come with knowing Brownie's death had been caused by the blow against the rock and not by having to save her.

It didn't come. Not yet. Maybe later, when she'd had time to digest what Callie had told her.

"I wish," she said slowly, "that someone had told me this sooner."

"I'm sorry," Callie said. "I guess I thought you knew. Other people knew . . ."

"But no one talked to me about it. No one talked to me about Brownie at all." Katie lifted her head. "Why is it," she asked Callie, "that people never talk about someone who died because they think it will be too painful? It's a lot more painful *not* talking about them."

Callie nodded. She stood up. "I'm sorry you didn't already know, Katie. But any time you want to talk about Brownie, you can talk to me. Okay?"

Katie nodded, grateful for the offer.

When Callie had gone, Katie lay back in bed, thinking. A rock? Brownie had hit his head on a rock?

There weren't any rocks sticking up out of the river. All the rocks were either at the bottom of the river or on the riverbank. And Brownie hadn't reached the bank.

Or . . . Katie's breath caught in her throat . . . or *had* he? Had he come *that* close to saving himself? That would explain how his wallet had ended up in the riverbank.

She had to find out where Davis got that picture he was carrying around in his wallet.

Dressing quickly in jeans and a Salem sweatshirt, Katie grabbed her books and left the room to look for Davis.

She didn't find him until noon.

He looked tired. She remembered then that he hadn't been home when she called his dorm the night before. Heavy date?

Pushing away the faint stirrings of jealousy caused by the thought, she asked him about the picture in his wallet.

"The one of me and Brownie," she explained as Davis reached into a pocket for his wallet. "The one Callie took. She said you have one, and I wondered where you got it. There were only two wallet-sized. Brownie had one, and I had the other one. So where did you get yours?"

He flipped the wallet open. "This the one you mean?" he asked.

Katie looked at the picture. Seeing it again was like being stabbed with a very sharp knife. "Yes. That's the one. Where did you get yours?" Encased in stiff, clear plastic as it was, it was hard for her to see if the picture looked as if it could have been in the river. And Davis *could* have cleaned it off.

"Brownie showed me the pictures Callie took that day. They were great, and I wanted a set, so I asked him for the negatives." Davis smiled at Katie. "They weren't the only ones who won that day, Katie. I won, too. While you were watching Brownie and Callie win at doubles, I was creaming Jon Shea. You know, from Nightmare Hall. He's good. It was a tough fight, but I beat him. So, I wanted a souvenir. Brownie said no problem, and gave me the negatives."

"Yes, but why did you have *this* picture made into a wallet size?"

The look of pain that she'd seen when she first came back to campus returned to Davis's eyes. "I miss him, too, Katie. He was my best friend. This was the best picture Callie took that day, and I liked the fact that you were in it, too. That seemed . . . right, somehow."

He sounded sincere. And he *had* been Brownie's best friend. She knew he missed him.

How *much* did he miss him? Enough to be really angry with the person he thought was responsible for his best friend's death?

Crazy thought. Davis wouldn't hurt her. He wouldn't stuff her into a plastic bag or try to drown her in a pool.

Would he?

When Davis left, Katie walked over and sat down on the low stone wall around the fountain.

People passing by said, "Hi, Katie," or "How's it going?" but she didn't answer. She only looked up after they'd passed, wondering as their backs moved away if those were the shoulders of a strong swimmer with an iron grip, if those were the arms of someone who had lifted her and dumped her into a white plastic prison. How could you tell if someone had the ability to kill?

"Brooding again?" Allen's voice said.

When she glanced up, he took a seat beside her. "Bad thoughts?" he asked gently.

"Why didn't you tell me Brownie hit his head on a rock?" Katie accused.

He looked shocked. "I thought you knew. Everyone thought you knew. You didn't?"

Katie shook her head. "I just found out. All this time, I thought he died because he was trying to save me. Callie just told me he was knocked unconscious when he hit his head on a rock."

"Must have been rough, finding out now." Allen took her hand in his. "I wondered why you were so quiet. Kind of like old times, seeing you sitting there so quietly . . ." There was a note of wistfulness in his voice that pained Katie. He missed Kit, did he? Too bad. She was gone forever. And good riddance!

To prove that Kit *was* gone, Katie suddenly

swung around and began scooping up handfuls of water, sloshing them in Allen's direction, soaking his clothes in seconds.

"Hey, cut it out!" He jumped up and away from the fountain. "I was nuts to sit down beside you. Should have known better. Even when you're depressed, it's still anything for a laugh, right?"

She was sorry immediately. After she'd promised herself she was going to make people take her seriously. "I'm . . . I'm sorry. I don't know what got into me."

"I do! You know, it really bothers me when you try to act like him. When are you going to wise up and realize that it just doesn't work for you?"

Davis had said almost the same thing.

"I'm sorry," she said again, and getting up, hurried off to her room.

She ran into Davis halfway there, but brushed past him without a word. All around her, students hurried across the rolling green lawns to class or campus activities, smiling, laughing, talking to friends. Having fun. Unafraid.

She had had that once. And now, she couldn't even remember what it had felt like.

When she reached her room, the first thing she did was lock the door. She had learned nothing today, nothing that would help her. Another day wasted. But . . . at least nothing terrible had happened. Maybe Callie would stay with her again tonight.

She had barely dropped her backpack when a knock sounded at the door. As she always did now, she asked, "Who is it?"

"Davis. Can I see you for a minute?"

She wasn't sure if she wanted to talk to him. What point was there in talking to someone who thought her mind was playing tricks on her?

But . . . she wouldn't mind talking a little bit more about that picture in Davis's wallet. Had Brownie really given him those negatives? Or had Davis found the wallet and removed Brownie's copy?

And where was that wallet now?

She let him in.

He sat on her desk chair, turning it so that he faced her. She sat on the bed.

"Look, Katie, something's going on and I want to know what it is. You barely spoke to me just now, out on the Commons. If I've done something, I want to know what it is. Is it the picture? The one in my wallet, of you and Brownie? Do you want it?"

"No. I already have one, I told you."

"They why don't you want *me* to have one?"

"I didn't say that. It's just . . . I told you, I thought there were only two copies."

"But I explained that."

"I know . . ."

"You don't believe me, do you?" Davis looked genuinely puzzled. "I don't get it. Why would you think I was lying about Brownie giving me the negatives?"

"It's just that I found his wallet," Katie explained, "and that picture was missing. So when Callie told me you had one, I . . ."

"You found Brownie's wallet? Where?"

"On the riverbank."

And Davis got it, then. She could see it in his face. He had guessed what she was wondering about. "You . . . you think I found the wallet, took the picture out and kept it, and then left the wallet there? Instead of giving it to Callie? Or to you? Why would I do that?"

She had never figured that out.

"I don't know what's going on here," Davis said, getting up, "but if seeing those negatives with Brownie's name on the envelope will get that I-don't-trust-you look off your face, it's worth a trip back to the dorm. *Don't* go anywhere. I want this settled." And he hurried out of the room.

Maybe he was going back to his dorm to get a weapon . . . a knife or even a gun.

He had seemed sincere. But then, he would, wouldn't he? If she bought it, and she trusted him, she'd let him get close enough to . . .

Talking about the pictures reminded her that Callie had given them each a set of pictures from that last day . . . the pictures Callie had taken with Brownie's camera. She had waited awhile until the wound wasn't quite so raw, until she thought they might be ready to see them. Katie had never worked up the courage to look at them.

Maybe it was time now. There could be something in the pictures from that day that would tell her something. Something she'd forgotten, something important . . .

It wasn't as painful as she'd thought it would be. Fortunately, Brownie wasn't in any of the pictures. That would have been agonizing, to see pictures of him laughing and horsing around that day, so shortly before he died. But the pictures were all of LuAnn and Davis, or Callie and Davis, or of LuAnn alone or Davis alone. And there were pictures of the woods, and of the river, running wild behind campus.

She went through them several times before she realized that Allen wasn't in a single picture. No surprise there. He hated having his picture taken. He'd been saying for years that he looked like a "dork" in pictures. He'd probably ducked or run every time Callie lifted the camera.

Callie must have been annoyed with him. She'd intended the pictures to be mementos of their outing, and she would have wanted at least one picture of all of them together in the woods. Maybe if she'd known what was coming, she wouldn't have cared if the day were immortalized on film or not.

When the phone rang, Katie was studying one of the pictures of the wild, rushing river, wondering whatever had possessed Brownie, thinking he could handle that angry water.

It was Callie, asking if Katie wanted to come upstairs and stay the night with her.

What a relief! She wouldn't have to be alone. Katie accepted enthusiastically, and then added, "I'm looking at the pictures you took . . . the ones of your hike that day. I hadn't looked at them before. Couldn't. But it's not so bad now. They're pretty good, except that Allen, as usual, hid from the camera. He's always done that. Camera-shy, big time."

"No, that's not why," Callie said. "There aren't any pictures of Allen because he wasn't with us."

"Sure, he was. Remember? Brownie and I . . . we got in the canoe, and Allen and you and

Davis and LuAnn headed into the woods."

"Right. But we'd only been walking a few minutes when Allen said he was getting a headache from the ragweed and had to go back to the dorm. And he did. That's why he's not in any of the pictures."

"He's allergic to ragweed." The thought came to Katie unbidden: "Did he walk back along the riverbank, do you know?"

"I don't think so. I think he took a shortcut through the woods. Why?"

She was thinking that if Allen had walked back along the riverbank, he might have seen something . . . might have seen Brownie fighting to get to shore . . . might know what had happened.

Wouldn't he have told her if he had?

No. If he'd witnesed Brownie's struggle and seen him lose the battle, he would never have described that scene to Katie, knowing it would devastate her. Allen wasn't cruel. He would never put her through that.

And he probably wouldn't tell her now.

But she *wanted* to know. Needed to know. If he'd seen anything, anything at all that would explain exactly what had happened, she wanted to know what it was.

Telling Callie she'd be right up, Katie hung up.

But before she went to Callie's, she had to see Allen. Throwing a few things in her backpack, Katie left the room and took the elevator up to Allen's room on the fourth floor.

The door was unlocked, but no one was there. The room was impeccably neat, as always. She had studied there with Allen at the beginning of the semester, when studying was still very important to her. Katie smiled. Allen couldn't study in her room now that it was such a mess. He couldn't stand to be in it for more than a few minutes.

Disappointed that he wasn't there, Katie glanced at the windows, rapidly darkening. If she went upstairs to Callie's right now, she'd be safe. She could talk to Allen tomorrow, after a good night's sleep. It would be insane to go looking for him out on campus, where she didn't even feel safe during the daylight hours.

But she needed to talk to him. She wouldn't be able to sleep at all tonight if she didn't see him first. He was probably at the library.

She had about fifteen minutes of daylight left. That might be enough time . . .

But if she was going to be running around outside looking for Allen, she'd need a heavier sweater. She'd just grab one of his, from the closet. He wouldn't mind. She'd borrowed his jackets and sweaters often in high school.

His closet, like Allen himself, was organized. She had to push aside a group of shirts to reach into the back for a sweater. . . .

At first, she thought she was dreaming. Or hallucinating. She couldn't be seeing what she was seeing. Couldn't be . . . not possible . . . insane. She really was losing her mind.

But . . . there it was, hanging on the wall behind Allen's neatly hung clothes, the clothes that Katie had pushed aside. Normally, with the clothes in place, it would be hidden. But not now. Now . . . it hung there, staring out at her. . . .

. . . A giant blowup of the picture of Brownie and Katie, smiling at each other . . . the picture that Callie had taken on the day of the tennis match, blown up to gigantic proportions. Katie's own smiling, happy face, bigger than life, was staring back at her from the closet wall.

But . . . not . . . Brownie's.

Because where Brownie's dark brown eyes and curly hair and devilish grin should have been, *Allen's* thin, serious face had been pasted into place.

Brownie's face had been cut out of the picture, and Allen's had been inserted in its place.

Nausea rose inside Katie. Horrible . . . horrible . . . why would Allen *do* such a horrible thing?

She began to back away, one hand over her mouth, her eyes disbelieving.

And from behind her, Allen's voice said softly, "Looking for something?"

Chapter 18

Katie whirled around to see Allen, an odd smile on his face, standing in front of the door to his own room. He had closed it.

"And did we find what we were looking for?" he asked, still smiling as he moved across the room to his desk. "It really isn't nice to go through other people's things. Shows a definite lack of good manners."

Lost in shock and confusion, Katie remained where she was, standing stock-still in front of Allen's closet. She could almost feel, on her back and shoulders, the eyes in the photograph behind her. "Where . . ." she cleared her throat and tried again, "where did you get that photograph? The one of Brownie and me? Did you . . . did you ask Brownie for the negatives, too? Like Davis?"

His back to her, Allen reached into a desk

drawer, extracted something, and turned around to face her.

At first, she thought she was seeing things. Maybe her friends had been right. Maybe she'd been seeing things all along.

Because that couldn't possibly be a long, nasty-looking knife in Allen's hands. What would Allen want with a knife?

But . . . it *was* a knife. With a very wide blade.

His smile widened. "Did I ask Brownie for the negatives? No, I did not ask Brownie for the negatives. I got that picture out of his wallet, dear heart. Then I cleaned your sweet little photo up a little, took it to the mall, and had the photo studio there do a blowup for me. Do you like it? It's pretty terrific, don't you think? Wasn't that expensive, either. And worth every penny I spent, if you ask me." He tilted his head. "And you *did* ask me, didn't you?"

Katie couldn't take her eyes off the knife. The closet light shone on the blade. It looked very, very sharp. "You . . . you found the wallet? And took the picture out? But . . . then you buried the wallet again? What for?"

Allen laughed. "Buried it *again*? I only buried it *once*. That was after I took it from Brownie and removed the picture."

Katie gasped. "You took it from . . . Brownie?"

"Is there an echo in this room? Listen carefully: I . . . took . . . the . . . picture . . . out of . . . Brownie's . . . wallet . . . and . . . buried . . . it. And *you* found it, didn't you? It was in your room. But you already *have* a wallet. An expensive red leather one that I myself gave Kit for her birthday. So I saw no reason for you to keep Brownie's. It's not as if anyone needs two wallets. I confiscated it. Hope you don't mind. Of course I burned it." Allen's laugh sounded like a cackle. "I mean, let's face it, he won't be needing it."

Katie struggled to remain calm. Staying calm would help her straighten things out. It was so confusing . . . the picture, that weird smile on Allen's face, the knife . . . "You . . . you couldn't have taken the wallet from Brownie. How could you? He . . . he . . ."

"Drowned is the word you're looking for. Brownie drowned. Dead, gone, kaput. But," Allen walked casually over to the door and leaned against it, "Brownie was such a good swimmer. You said so yourself, many times. Everyone assumed he never made it to the riverbank, that the current took hold of the poor lad and held him prisoner until he died, his lungs full of water."

"It . . . did."

"No, ma'am, it did *not*. That nasty old river had some help along the way." He stopped talking then and grinned at her, lazily flicking the knife back and forth.

And it occurred to Katie then that she wasn't surprised. Hadn't she always known that Brownie was too strong a swimmer to let that river defeat him? But . . . but Callie had said that Brownie'd hit his head on a rock. "What are you talking about?" she asked, her voice little more than a whisper.

"He made it to the riverbank." Allen left the door then and came to stand directly in front of Katie. Instinctively, she tried to back away, but there was nowhere to go except the closet. The knife was right there, in Allen's right hand . . . much too close. . . .

"He did make it to the riverbank," Allen repeated. "But then, something happened."

She didn't want to know what had happened. Her stomach began to rise against her, and a little vein in her temple began tapping out an anxious rhythm.

Allen stroked the tip of the knife with one finger. "Poor old Brownie's head slammed into a rock." He laughed again. "A rock in my *hand*." He shook his head. "He was beat from fighting that nasty current. Lay there like a dying fish. But I could tell he was about to get his second wind and climb up to dry land, and I couldn't have that, could I? I just couldn't have that." He lifted the knife-wielding arm over his head and then brought it down in one strong, angry thrust. "So, *boom*! Skull met rock and that was all she wrote."

Katie's legs turned to water and she slid to the floor. "No, no," she murmured, her head lolling on her shoulders, "no, you didn't . . ."

"Oh, yes, I *did*!" he shouted, crouching low to shove his face close to hers. "He ruined everything! I never knew what Kit saw in him! Conceited, show-offy . . . he thought he was such hot stuff, and Kit fell all over him. She was supposed to be with *me* when we got to college. Everyone knew that. My parents, Kit's parents, our friends . . . maybe we were just pals in high school, but I knew it would be different when we got to college. We'd be adults finally . . . no more high school stuff . . . and I was sure she'd see me differently away from home. I figured she'd finally be ready to admit that we belonged together. Forever." Allen glared at the floor, as if it were somehow responsible. "And then she met Brownie, and everything changed."

Katie's mind, fogged by shock and disbelief, wondered why he was talking about her in the third person. He kept saying, "Kit." But *she* was Kit.

"You killed him," she whispered through numbed lips.

"I did," he said, nodding. "I did do that." Suddenly, he reached over and grabbed her left arm. "Get up!" he shouted. "Get up right now!" And he dragged her to her feet.

She couldn't stand. Her legs wouldn't hold her up. Allen was forced to, clutching her around the waist, forcing her to stay on her feet.

That grip . . . that iron grip around her waist . . .

Katie lifted her head and stared at him. "You . . . in the pool . . . it was you . . ."

He grinned down at her. "Right again. Give the lady a gold star. I don't understand why your grades are so bad. You obviously have a keen, analytical mind. Also me in the attic at Nightmare Hall, to save you more guessing. I thought the garment bag was a nice touch, didn't you?" His grin widened. "Want to know where it is? Inside one of the other bags, folded up and lying on the bottom. You checked the outside of the bags, but you didn't check the inside. Your mistake. And just for your information, I did *not* hit you on the head. You did that yourself. There should be a sign in that closet warning people to watch out for low-hanging rafters, right?"

Katie's head was spinning. Allen had *killed* Brownie? And had tried to kill *her*? Allen was her . . . executioner? No, that couldn't be. She couldn't have been that wrong about someone. Allen had never in all the years she'd known him shown the slightest sign of . . . of anger or violence or cruelty . . . never. He was kind and gentle.

Then, in her mind's eye, she saw Brownie lying on the riverbank, exhausted, gasping for breath, saw Allen walk over and pick up a huge rock, saw him lift it over Brownie's head, saw him. . . .

She sagged against Allen and was repulsed by the very feel of him. But when she tried to recoil backward, he tightened his grip around her waist. He held the knife close to her throat, saying, "If you make a single sound, so much as a whimper, you're going to join Brownie right here and now."

"I don't understand," she whispered, "I don't understand . . ."

"What is it exactly that you fail to comprehend?" he asked sarcastically, beginning to drag her toward the door.

"If . . . if you killed Brownie because you wanted *me* . . . if that's true . . . why did you try to kill *me* in the attic and in the pool? That doesn't make any sense."

Horror flooded Allen's pale, thin face. "*You?* I don't want you! Why would I want *you*?"

They were almost to the door. Allen moved the knife from her throat and pushed it instead into her back, up underneath her sweater. Where, she knew, it wouldn't be seen by anyone who wasn't looking very closely. But . . . *she* would know it was there.

"But you said . . ." she was so confused, so terrified, her brain seemed to be moving through molasses. "You said Brownie ruined things for you with Kit. Isn't that what you said?"

"Yes. That *is* what I said. What's that got to do with you?"

He was standing slightly behind her, looking down into her face. And he was puzzled, she could see that. He really was puzzled.

"Allen," she said, her voice quaking, "you said you loved Kit, that you wanted Kit, and Brownie got in the way. But I *am* Kit. So why . . . why did you try to kill *me*?"

And then she watched in horrified awe as his face turned scarlet, his eyes bulged, and he screamed down into her face, "You are not Kit! Don't you dare say that! Don't you dare! You're *Katie*, and you aren't anything like Kit! She would never do the things you've done, act the way you act. I *hate* you, because you *killed* her, you killed Kit, you took her away from me, and I'll never forgive you for that. Never!"

Paralyzed by his awful rage, Katie had to struggle to find her voice. "You . . . you hate me for killing . . . *Kit*?"

"Well, of course I do! I waited for her to come back after she went home for two weeks. I knew she'd get over Brownie. And then she'd turn to me. But . . . she never *came* back." He glared ferociously at her. "*You* came instead. After everything I'd done for her, after I'd picked up that rock and bashed in Brownie's skull for her, and even though I didn't like him, it was still really, really hard to do. After all that, she never even came *back*. *You* came instead. I hung around and I waited and I waited," he was crying now, tears streaming down his cheeks, "but every time I thought maybe she was back, it always turned out to be *you*. Noisy and show-offy and reckless and careless, just like *him*!" His voice rose to an angry wail, "I *hated* that! I hated that so much! I couldn't *stand* it! It was like he wasn't really gone, after all. And Kit *was*!"

"I . . . I didn't — "

He clamped a hand roughly over her mouth. "Shut *up*! Just shut up! I don't care what you think you did or didn't. You *killed* my Kit. And you have to be punished. So I," he fumbled with the doorknob, "I put you on trial, right here in this room. And I weighed all of the evidence very carefully. And when I'd finished, there was no other verdict possible. Guilty. You were guilty of murdering Kit Sullivan, and that's all there was to it." His voice calmed as he opened the door. "I had no choice. Guilty, guilty, couldn't possibly reach any other verdict."

Katie muttered from behind his hand, "You wrote GUILTY on my car. Not Callie, you . . . you left the theater that night? I didn't know that. . . ."

"Well, how could you? You weren't in your own seat for more than five seconds at a time. Yeah, I wrote it. I wanted you to know that someone was onto you. That someone knew what you'd *done*."

"But . . . but I thought they meant that I was guilty for . . . for panicking and making Brownie save me, and then letting him drown."

"Well, you were wrong, weren't you?" He dragged her out into the hall. "Brownie deserved to die. But Kit didn't."

There had to be someone in the hall, Katie thought desperately. There *had* to! Someone, anyone . . .

There was no one in the hall. It stretched ahead of them, long and empty, dimly lit, doors to the other rooms closed, stereos blasting . . . no one would hear her even if she somehow managed to scream before Allen slit her throat.

"And of course," he said, dragging her along the hallway toward the stairwell door, "there wasn't any question about what your sentence would be. How many choices are there when it comes to murder? And it *was* premeditated, you know it was. You deliberately planned the extinction of the most important person in my life."

They were only a few feet away from the stairwell door. There wouldn't be anyone on the stairs, Katie was sure of that. Everyone used the elevators. She and Allen would go down eight flights without seeing a soul. And then . . . what?

"So," Allen announced, pulling the heavy metal door open and pushing her into the dim, musty stairwell, "there was only one sentence I could hand down."

She didn't want to hear what that sentence was.

"Death," he announced with satisfaction as he yanked her down the first few steps, "your sentence for murdering Kit Sullivan is death."

Chapter 19

Just as Katie had feared, they met no one on the stairs. With the tip of the knife pressed against her back, Katie went slowly from step to step. If she stumbled or hesitated for even an instant, Allen pushed her roughly, propelling her downward.

She glanced over her shoulder only once. The dim lighting illuminating the staircases turned Allen's face a sickly yellowish hue. His eyes, too, seemed to hold a cruel yellow light, like a wild animal caught in someone's flashlight. His full lips were clamped together with determination.

She wasn't going to be able to talk him out of this one. In high school, they had been so close, had such intimate talks.

But he would never listen to her now. It was *Kit* Sullivan he'd listened to, not Katie. He hated Katie. Nothing *she* could say would move him.

And that was when she realized that Allen had never, not once, called her "Katie." Everyone else had, after a while, when they'd realized she was serious about no longer being called "Kit." But not Allen. He hadn't continued to call her "Kit," because he knew she would have refused to answer. He simply hadn't called her by name at all.

Why hadn't she noticed?

But even if she had, she would have chalked it up to stubbornness on his part. Not anger . . . anger wouldn't have occurred to her. At least, not the kind of anger that would lead someone to kill.

They reached the basement door. So soon . . . she didn't want to leave the safety of the building. It was dark outside. Everything seemed so much worse in the dark.

Allen pulled the door open and pushed her outside. They emerged into a dark, deserted alleyway behind the Quad. There was no one around. No one to help her . . .

"Where are you taking me?" she asked.

"Didn't I tell you to shut up? I'm sure I did. Why don't you listen?" He had one hand on her bruised elbow. His other hand kept the knife in her back, the tip pressed against her skin just to the left of her backbone. "Oh, I forgot," he said, "Katie Sullivan does as she pleases, right? Doesn't listen to anyone. Nobody can tell *her* anything!"

"No, I — "

A hiss: "I *said* shut up!" The knife blade pricked her skin. It hurt.

She fell silent.

Where *was* everyone? Was there a game? A party? A dance? Why wasn't she there, in that other place where everyone was safely gathered, having fun?

This couldn't be Allen, pushing her along through the dark with a knife at her back. The Allen she had gone to school with, had studied with in her family's living room, had gone to movies and parties and dances with, *that* Allen had read poetry and listened to classical music and played the violin and basketball and had never lifted his hand in anger against another human being. Never even had a fight in the schoolyard. He had played ball in the backyard with her little brother Matt, and given her dog Rompers a bath, coaxing and cajoling the poodle the entire time in a soft, soothing voice.

What had *happened* to him?

You happened to him, a voice in her head accused. *You* did this!

But her own voice cried out then, surprising

her with its strength: *No!* No more guilt! *I* didn't kill Brownie, I wasn't responsible . . . he *did* make it to the riverbank and would have saved himself if it hadn't been for Allen. And I'm *not* responsible for what Allen has become. *Allen* is! Only Allen . . .

Suddenly, as they came out of the shadow of the Quad and moved to the rear of campus, he began singing, "Row, row, row your boat, gently down the stream. Merrily, merrily, merrily, merrily, you hit your head on a beam. Row, row, row, your boat, gently down the stream. Merrily, merrily, merrily, merrily, you'll never make the swim team."

His laughter rang out, cutting into the silence around them.

"I was disappointed when you didn't die in the attic. Nightmare Hall is such a great place for an execution. Oh, well, I'm flexible. I've thought of an even better place."

And in the next minute, she realized where he was taking her.

To the river. . . .

Allen was taking her to the river, where he meant to kill her.

She was going to die in the water. Like . . .

Like Brownie.

Chapter 20

Katie's eyes searched the darkness in desperation for someone to help her. She could hear shouts and occasional music in the distance, too far away to do her any good. No one ever roamed around behind campus this late at night, she knew that. All those nights that she'd come down here alone, she hadn't run into anyone. And had been glad of it, knowing that they'd have give her questioning looks and wondered what she was doing there all by herself so late at night.

But no one had ever come along, and no one would tonight, either, she was sure of it. There was just Allen, who meant to kill her.

Brownie had saved her before when she had almost died in the river. But Brownie was gone. Who would save her this time?

She expected Allen to aim for the canoe landing. Instead, he turned and began pulling her toward the old railroad bridge, looming across the river like a giant black sculpture. Trains hadn't traveled across the metal bridge in a long time. Students at Salem were warned against using it to cross to the woods on the other side due to the deterioration of the structure. It wasn't safe, they had been told.

Yet that was where Allen was headed.

The tip of the knife remained firmly pressed against Katie's back.

When they reached the bridge, Allen pushed her roughly away from him, up against the wide black support that held up a narrow black metal railing spanning the length of the bridge. Katie could hear the water slapping gently along the shore below the riverbank.

"Well?" Allen said, "what are you waiting for?"

Dumbfounded, she looked at him. The dark shadow of Butler Hall, Salem's administration building, loomed behind him in the distance. It seemed smaller now, from where Katie was standing. "I'm . . . I'm waiting for you to let me go!" she said defiantly, thrusting her chin out as far as it would go. "This is dumb, Allen. You're *not* a judge or a jury. You don't get to say who's guilty and who isn't."

He waved the knife at her. The light from the half moon above danced on the silver blade.

"Let you go? Okay, I'll let you go." He pointed to the skinny bridge railing. "Right up there. You can go right up there."

Katie glanced sideways, at the railing. It was narrower than the width of her sneakered foot. "On the railing? Allen, it's not wide enough. I can't . . ."

His voice lowered dangerously as he thrust the blade up under her chin. "Is this Katie Sullivan saying 'can't'? The reckless, carefree Katie Sullivan who climbs fire escapes and dances in fountains?" He pulled the knife away. "I'll make a deal with you. You walk all the way across the bridge on that railing, and I'll let you go. Fair enough?"

Fair? She wouldn't make it more than a few inches without falling, and they both knew it. If she fell into the water, she'd die, and if she fell onto the surface of the bridge, Allen would kill her with the knife. "Heads I lose, tails I lose," she mumbled.

He heard her. "Figured that out, did you?" He laughed. "Well, that's the way it goes, right? At least, I'm giving you a chance. Lots of judges wouldn't. Anyway, this *is* Katie Sullivan I'm talking to, right? Seems to me this is just the kind of crazy stunt Katie Sullivan loves. Too bad there's no audience around except me. I know how you love a crowd. Look, tell you what, I'll clap and yell as loud as I can, okay? That way, you can pretend I'm a crowd."

When she didn't move or answer him, he began prodding her with the knife, pushing the tip of it against her neck. And his voice changed, became colder, angrier. "I . . . said . . . climb *up* . . . there. *Now!*"

Katie tried to back away from him, but the railing stopped her. "I . . . I can't! I'll fall, Allen, you know I will. The fall alone will probably kill me. Even if it doesn't, I'll get hurt too badly to swim. I'll . . . I'll drown."

"Perfect!" he sang out. "*You* drowned Kit. When you came out of the river that day, there wasn't any more Kit. So this is what I call perfect justice. Now quit stalling, and get up there on that railing. Or I'll kill you right here and now."

She knew he meant it.

Forbidding herself to look down at the dark water below, Katie turned toward the railing. Clutching the thick, black metal side beam with both hands, she pulled herself up, as if she were climbing onto a balance beam. "I can't see," she complained as a thick, black cloud covered the half moon.

"And you've somehow convinced yourself that I care?" Allen said lazily. But he remained vigilantly by her side, the knife still in his hand.

"Too bad you're not wearing high heels," he added. "That would make it so much more interesting."

When she had both feet planted on the railing, Katie had to cling to an overhead support to remain upright. But that support would only be within her reach for another few seconds before slanting away at such an angle that her fingertips wouldn't be able to touch it. Then what would she hold onto?

"If you fall," Allen said, his voice soft and menacing, "everyone will think it was suicide. We all know how freaked out you've been since Brownie's death. Doing stupid things, taking crazy chances, as if you were testing Fate. Trying to see what it would take to end your *own* life. No one will be the least bit surprised when you're found floating in the river."

"I have *never* been suicidal," Katie declared hotly. "Never! No one will believe it."

"They wouldn't have believed it of Kit. But they will of you. We all saw you climb that fire escape. What was that if it wasn't suicidal?" Allen poked at her ankles with the tip of the knife. "That was when I knew Kit was gone forever. I'd been hoping it was only temporary, the result of your precious boyfriend dying. I was willing to wait. But watching you climb that rickety old fire escape, I knew Kit was never coming back. She would never have done something so crazy. I hated you more that day than I've ever hated anyone. And that's when I knew it was hopeless."

"So you turned to Callie?" Katie's voice shook. "She loves you, Allen. But she'll never forgive you for killing her brother. Never!"

"What I'm doing," he said calmly, "has nothing to do with Callie. This is unfinished business between you and me. And Callie's never going to know about Brownie. *You're* not going to be around to tell her, are you? And I see no need to tell her. Ever." He laughed, a low, evil chuckle. "Wouldn't Brownie turn over in his grave if he knew his sister was in love with me? That's part of Callie's charm, frankly. That she was his sister, and that he'd hate her dating the guy who bashed in his skull. The icing on the cake, if you know what I mean."

Sickened, Katie stopped listening. The overhead support had slanted away from her now. She had to let go. And it took every ounce of concentration to balance on the skinny railing, her arms outstretched on either side of her, her feet taking the tiniest of tiny steps, in a slow, careful shuffle. The knife point repeatedly jabbed at her legs, prodding her forward each time she hesitated.

She could hear the water swishing along beneath her. Then the half moon slid out from behind the cloud and dappled the black river with silver ribbons. It looked cold, and deep. And unless she did something to save herself, it was going to become her watery grave.

It was *Katie* Allen was intent on killing. Not Kit, never Kit.

Well, *she* was Kit, wasn't she? Had been. Still was, in a way. If she could convince Allen of that, she might have a chance.

But she could hardly remember what Kit was like. Quiet, not loud and brassy. Competent, capable, responsible. None of that mattered now. But . . . Kit was also not terribly brave . . . a little shy, frightened of many things . . . how would she have reacted to being forced to walk a skinny little metal railing high above the river?

Easy answer: she'd have been paralyzed with fear. No problem there. No acting experience required.

"I can't move," Katie said breathlessly, changing her voice, returning to Kit's soft, unsure quality. "Allen, I can't move!" She didn't have to fake the terror in her words.

The voice alone startled him. She saw it in the way he jerked upright, out of his confident slouch against the railing. "What?" he cried.

Concentrating on keeping the helplessness

in her voice, Katie said, "I can't do this, Allen. Help me, please, please, help me! I'm going to fall. You won't let me fall, will you, Allen? Please don't let me fall." She finished on a sob. It took no effort to do so.

Glancing down and sideways, she found him looking up at her, bewilderment on his face.

She pressed her advantage. "Allen, remember when we were decorating for the senior prom, and I had to climb that ladder to hang the fake clouds? I panicked and froze, and couldn't climb back down. You came up to get me and help me down, remember? I was crying, I was so scared, and you kept saying, 'It's okay, Kit, I'm coming, I'm coming.' You calmed me down and then you helped me get back down the ladder. Remember, Allen?"

"Kit?" he asked, and although there was disbelief in his voice, she could feel how badly he wanted to believe.

"And when you were teaching me to drive," she rushed on, her balance on the railing wavering a bit as she concentrated on sounding exactly like Kit, "remember? It started snowing like mad that one Saturday. I panicked when the car started sliding all over the road, and I froze behind the wheel. Remember that day, Allen? You helped me steer and you talked me through it, all the way home. I couldn't have made it if you hadn't been there."

"Kit," he breathed, staring up at her in wonder, "is that really you?" She could hear the suspicion in his voice waning. He wanted, so very much, to believe her.

"Graduation night," she continued, fighting dizziness, "remember graduation night? Don Grady had too much to drink and made a pass at me outside of school, and you came out just in time and told him to buzz off, and he did. I couldn't have handled him, Allen, not by myself. Every time I got into trouble, you were there to help me." The dizziness threatened to overwhelm her. "Help me now, Allen, *please*. Help me down from here, before I fall." She kept that sad, pleading note in her voice through every word, as Kit would have done.

"It *is* you," he said then. "Kit, you're *back*!"

Katie had been using so much concentration on her charade that she had left very little for maintaining her balance, and she began to teeter on the railing.

Seeing her waver dangerously, Allen dropped the knife and grabbed a beam, prepared to climb onto the railing. The weapon slipped between two metal strips on the floor of the bridge and disappeared. It was gone.

Katie breathed a little easier.

Allen didn't seem to notice. He was already climbing onto the railing, words spilling out of him, words of relief and joy. "Oh, Kit, I can't believe it, I thought you were gone for good, I thought you'd never come back. I'm sorry I scared you, but if I'd known this was all it would take to get you back . . . Here, let me help you down." There was relief and gratitude and happiness in his voice. "And I don't care about Callie, Kit. I don't. Now that you're back . . ."

Now he would get her down, Katie thought with relief. Without the knife, he wouldn't be able to stop her from running. She would race for campus, screaming at the top of her lungs for help. Even if he caught up with her, the fight would be much more equal without the knife.

But first, she had to get down off the railing. He had to help her.

"Kit, I've missed you so much," Allen whispered as he reached out for her. He was taller than she was, and could reach the slanting metal beam to his left. Clutching that with one hand for support, he reached for her with the other hand.

And then she made a fatal mistake. Looking

into his face, she saw him on the riverbank that day, saw him bend to lift a heavy rock, saw him heft it over the head of Brownie, lying exhausted in the mud, saw him smash it down . . .

And as Allen reached out to save her, she recoiled in revulsion, jerking away from him.

He knew instantly. And he was furious. "You tricked me!" he screamed, his face twisting with rage. "You're not Kit! You're still Katie! You tricked me!" Still holding the beam with his left hand, his right hand slapped out at her . . . but now, not to *save* her. To *push* her . . . off the railing and down, down, into that dark, deep, cold water.

Knowing she was lost, Katie, with nothing to hold onto, reached for the only thing available to her . . . Allen's arm.

As he slapped at her, she grabbed his jacket sleeve and clutched it with both hands, even as she lost her balance totally and began to fall sideways . . . but not toward the floor of the bridge. She was falling in the other direction, toward the river below.

And although Allen screamed in rage, Katie did *not* let go of the sleeve. She hung on with every ounce of strength and when the full weight of her body left the railing, it pulled on Allen's arm with enough force to destroy his own balancing act. He let out an angry shout as his left arm was ripped away from the beam.

He was still shouting as they toppled off the bridge as a pair, falling, falling, toward the dark water below.

Chapter 21

Hitting the water was a bone-numbing shock. It was cold, colder than Katie would have thought possible, and the force of the fall sent her down, down, straight down into its murky depths.

It was an even greater shock to realize, as awareness hit her slowly, that she was . . . alive! The fall hadn't killed her, the impact when her body slammed into the water hadn't killed her . . . she was alive! If her legs or ankles were broken, she felt no pain. And what did it matter, anyway? She wasn't *dead*.

It wasn't until she returned to the surface and began gulping in air that she realized she was no longer clutching Allen's sleeve. Had they separated on the way down? Or after they hit the water?

Alive . . . alive . . .

Was Allen alive, too?

Katie's heart began pounding wildly. If he was alive, *where* was he? He could be somewhere below her, as he'd been in the campus pool . . . about to grab her ankles in that same iron-fisted grip and yank her beneath the surface again.

Propelled by fear, she began swimming frantically toward shore. The water was shallower now, quieter than it had been when the canoe had overturned. That seemed a million years ago now, another time, another place. She had been so frightened to find herself in the river. Paralyzed by fear, panicked into helplessness.

Not *this* time. There was no one here now, no one to help her but herself. Katie had to save Katie.

She could *do* it. If Allen didn't suddenly swim up from nowhere and drag her back down, she could save herself. Because Allen had been right about one thing: Kit Sullivan *had* died in the river that day. And the Katie who had survived thought life was far too short not to fight for every single minute.

Maybe she wouldn't make it to shore. Maybe she'd die trying. But, like Brownie, she *would* die trying. It hadn't been his fault he hadn't made it all the way. It had been Allen's fault. And it wouldn't be hers, either, if she didn't make it. She'd give it all she had.

So she stroked through the cold, black water, awkwardly at first, then more smoothly, her arms slicing through the silver-ribboned water with determination fueled by anger at Allen. He had taken Brownie's life, deliberately and cruelly, and then he had planned to end *hers*. Not tonight, Allen, she thought as she pulled closer to shore. I'm still alive, see me swimming? And I plan to stay that way for a very long time. Live with it.

Small black figures on the riverbank appeared through the darkness. They seemed to be shouting, and waving.

And although she was exhausted and her legs had begun to throb with pain, Katie found herself hoping that no one would jump in to help her. It suddenly seemed terribly important that she make her own way to shore.

Stroke, stroke . . . so cold, so wet, so tired . . . stroke, stroke . . . hard to breathe, chest hurting . . . no sign of Allen, no frantic thrashing sounds behind her, no cries for help. Allen had never been a very good swimmer.

Stroke, stroke . . . not my fault Brownie died, not my fault. Allen's fault . . . Not guilty. I'm not guilty! Brownie would have made it safely to shore if Allen hadn't hit him with the rock.

The thought gave her renewed strength, and minutes later she was lying on the riverbank and Davis and Callie were rushing to help her. Davis covered her with something . . . a sweater? Callie wiped her face and hair with a soft cloth . . . a handkerchief? a scarf? Someone called, "LuAnn, go call an ambulance!" and feet quickly padded away.

"Allen," Katie gasped, "Allen . . . still in the water?"

"No," Davis said, sitting on the grass and laying her head in his lap. "He's lying over there. Out cold. Made it to the riverbank, and then passed out. The police will take care of him."

"The police? How did you . . . ?"

"Davis suspected Allen," Callie volunteered softly. Her face was white with shock, her eyes filled with tears. "I still can't believe it. I . . . I loved him . . . and he *killed* my brother. I feel so sick . . ."

"You didn't know," Katie whispered. "None of us did, Callie." She turned her head toward Davis. "Why did *you* suspect him?"

"I knew how strongly Allen felt about you before. He seemed to really resent the way you'd changed. I saw him watching you, and I finally realized what he was watching for were signs that you were still *Kit*. Then, when I saw that word written on your car, I remembered that Allen had left the theater during the movie. I checked out his right hand. It was dirty, dusty."

Davis took Katie's hands in his. "Allen's hand shouldn't have been dirty if he'd been sitting in the theater watching a movie the whole time. I wasn't sure what he thought you were guilty of, but I figured it had something to do with the way you'd changed. I tried to keep an eye on him, but he kept giving me the slip. At Nightmare Hall, he wasn't downstairs with the rest of us when you were trapped in that garment bag. When I asked him about it later, he said he'd been out back, checking out the creek behind the house. But his shoes weren't muddy."

"Last night, Davis sat outside your room all night long," Callie said. "He was afraid Allen would try something." Her eyes, still full of shock and disbelief, kept returning to the spot where Allen lay, unconscious.

"That's why you weren't there when I called," Katie told Davis. "I thought . . ."

Davis nodded. "I know. It's okay. I don't blame you for anything you thought. Forget it."

"But you . . ." Katie kept her head in his lap. It felt warm and safe. "I thought you didn't believe me when I told you about the attic. You acted as if you didn't. Like you thought I was losing my grip."

"I know. I feel bad about that. But I was still trying to figure out what was going on. And I didn't want to say anything until I was sure. I figured I'd get some proof and then I'd go to the police, and it'd be over. But," he added ruefully, "I underestimated our friend Allen."

Katie felt an overwhelming need to close her eyes and sleep. But first . . . "How did you know where we were?"

"I went to your room to bring you the negatives, and you weren't there. So I went to Allen's room looking for you. Your backpack was lying on the floor, as if you'd dropped it in a hurry. And the closet door was open. I saw the picture he'd blown up, Katie, and I knew I'd been right. That's really sick."

"It was my idea to look for you at the river," Callie said quietly. "Allen was fixated on this river. I thought it was because . . ." her voice faltered ". . . because it had taken Brownie from us. I didn't realize that Allen didn't care anything about that. He was fixated on it because when you came out of the river that day, you weren't Kit anymore. So when Davis called me and asked if I had any idea where you and

Allen might be, I knew right away to come here first."

The knowledge that Davis and Callie had been out looking for her warmed Katie, especially since Callie must have been devastated when Davis told her what he suspected about Allen. Katie had felt so alone. And she hadn't really been alone, after all.

Except . . . in the river, she had been alone. And that was okay. She had been scared . . . more scared than she'd ever been before. But she had kept going. She had saved her own life. Although she knew she'd always miss Brownie, at last she was free of the guilt.

Pretty Please

Several years earlier . . .

It's such a nice day. A pretty day. The sun is shining. I wonder what it would feel like on my face. Warm, I think.

I wish I could go outside. There are other kids out there, I can hear them. They're laughing and shouting and they sound like they're having so much fun. Their school is out for the summer and they're so glad to be on vacation. I wish I could be on vacation with them.

I wonder what it's really like outside? In the daytime, I mean. I wish They'd let me go out before dark.

But I know They're right. If They didn't love me, if They didn't care about me, They'd let me go out. And then everyone would laugh at me and call me names and run away from me. That would hurt so bad. That would hurt more than it hurts me to look into a mirror. And that hurts a lot.

I shouldn't complain. It could be a lot worse. Like They say, I could have been born to people who didn't care about me, who didn't mind if I got hurt, people who would let me go outside and be treated cruelly. I'm very lucky to have Them. They protect me. They always have. And they always will.

She said They're getting me a video game for my eleventh birthday. So I'll have something new and interesting to do.

I'm really grateful to Them. I love Them very much. Sometimes I think I hate Them, but I make those bad thoughts go away.

Because why would I hate Them?

About the Author

"Writing tales of horror makes it hard to convince people that I'm a nice, gentle person," says **Diane Hoh**.

"So what's a nice woman like me doing scaring people?

"Discovering the fearful side of life: what makes the heart pound, the adrenalin flow, the breath catch in the throat. And hoping always that the reader is having a frightfully good time, too."

Diane Hoh grew up in Warren, Pennsylvania. Since then, she has lived in New York, Colorado, and North Carolina, before settling in Austin, Texas. "Reading and writing take up most of my life," says Hoh, "along with family, music, and gardening." Her other horror novels include *Funhouse*, *The Accident*, *The Invitation*, *The Fever*, and *The Train*.